BAILEY'S IRISH DREAM
BOOK FOUR IN THE ANGEL CHRONICLES SERIES

ESTER LÓPEZ

Writing & Photographic Services LLC

For all my former co-workers at my favorite brewery and my favorite hotel

IN THE BEGINNING, MAY 2007

Bailey Jackson settled in her seat on the plane. She closed her eyes and prayed. *I'm coming to Ireland, Shaun. I hope to find you, to see if you are real. Please be real.*

Hello, love. I am real. I hope to meet you, too, her dream lover answered. She allowed the same erotic dream she'd had for the past year to take over. Bailey's pulse raced at the thought of actually meeting her dream lover. In her dreams, she was totally uninhibited, but in reality, that was not the case. When she awoke, she glanced at the passenger beside her. Hopefully, she hadn't talked in her sleep.

When the Aer Lingus jet landed at the Shannon Airport, she was eager to get to her destination in Roundstone. There, she would start the search for her dream lover, unofficially of course.

She was with a team of Hudson Inn employees, along with the owner. Their mission was to train new staff in Ireland and help set up the new hotel. The owner, Larry

Keith, was partner with an Irish businessman, new to the hotel industry. Part of the deal for Larry was that he would also manage the property. Larry had a track record for his current property, which made him millions.

Bailey jumped at the opportunity when Larry asked for volunteers. After all, she would be able to do research for her book while she was in Ireland. At least, that's what she kept telling herself.

She straightened her clothes and ran a hand over her shoulder-length hair to make sure she was presentable. "Hey, Linda, we're here," she said to the passenger beside her. She collected her computer bag and camera bag and waited for Linda to collect her belongings as well. She kept her passport, Visa, and wallet in her camera bag to eliminate the need for a purse. Too many things to carry.

She followed Linda off the plane. The air was quite chilly and she had a summer outfit on. She would have to find something warmer to wear and soon. Before Bailey left east Tennessee, her friend, Kay, had told her some things to expect when she arrived in Ireland, but she didn't mention the difference in the temperatures. This was her first trip abroad and she was nervous, anxious, and excited all at the same time. The eight-hour flight was bad enough with the crying baby, but with little sleep, except for her recurring dream, she pushed on. She had no other option.

During the trip, she and Linda had been separated from the rest of the team while on the plane. She found her team mates near the luggage area. Once she collected her things, she moved along with the group through Customs and exchanged her money for Euros.

Thank God they spoke English here, but she really had to concentrate when others spoke to her because the accent was so thick, it was hard to understand what they said. Finally, she located the bus that would take her and her team to their stop.

Larry announced that he had a rental car and would join them at the hotel later.

Hopping the bus to Roundstone, she sat next to Linda and pulled out her notebook, jotting down thoughts about the countryside and her experiences so far. This would do for a start. Writing a romance about a couple in Ireland needed descriptions and impressions of people and places. She wanted it to sound authentic.

"What are you writing there?" Linda asked.

"I'm just taking notes of my first impressions. I want to savor my time here."

Linda leaned back and closed her eyes. "I choose to catch up on the lost sleep," she said.

"Oh, I'm too excited right now for sleep." Bailey glanced out the window and realized it was still early morning, but how early? She glanced at her watch, but it had stopped. She totally forgot to buy a new battery. She spent one day just leaving the States and another eight hours of flight over the ocean to get to Ireland. She remained awake the entire time, except while she dreamed of Shaun. That's the name she gave her dream lover. This weird feeling must be the 'jet lag' she heard people talk about.

When the bus finally pulled to their stop, she collected her items and waited for the others before heading up the hill to the hotel. The excitement welled up inside her. She looked forward to sleeping in the Hudson bed.

Ted Carmichael, the head of maintenance, Maria Ortiz, the head housekeeper, and Linda Padron, the head of breakfast, climbed the hill beside her. She was experienced in working all three shifts at the hotel's front desk, even though she wasn't a manager. Her Front Desk Manager had decided to stay in the States.

She glanced at her watch again, forgetting it had stopped, when she reached the entrance to the hotel. She would have to buy a new battery and set it to Ireland time once she knew what time it really was.

There were workers outside on the scaffolding, applying finishing touches to the front of the hotel. Inside, there were workers putting up wallpaper around the lobby. The lobby was huge, with no furniture at the moment.

"I think I'll check out the place," Ted said. He left his bags beside the group and walked off to speak to some of the wallpaper hangers.

"That looks like it could be the kitchen," Linda said. She left her bags and walked toward a door at the far end of the lobby area.

"Well, I'm not interested in seeing any rooms except my own right now," Maria said. "I'm tired."

Bailey scratched her head. She agreed with Maria. She was getting tired now that some of the excitement had worn off. Researching her book was the excuse she had given her three adult children before leaving her home in the Smoky Mountains.

"Mom, I really don't think you should be going to Ireland by yourself," her daughter had said.

"Don't you think it's a little early to be doing this? You know, so soon after dad...died," her youngest son had said.

"How long will you be gone?" her eldest son asked when he realized he couldn't change her mind.

Being married to a verbally abusive man for over 26 years kept the woman she was from becoming the woman she was meant to be.

Besides, her husband had been dead for a year now, and

while he was alive, she spent all her time and energy defending herself against his abusive language and trying to keep a positive attitude. She spent many nights crying herself to sleep. Since his death, she found the time and energy to write and be creative. It was refreshing and gave her hope for a brighter future. She didn't find time to miss him with her two jobs, and she certainly didn't miss his verbal abuse.

After a short wait, Larry showed up. "Mr. Shaunessy will meet us later today. Let's synchronize our watches." Bailey checked her phone since her watch was useless, but discovered she had no service. She realized she would have to do something about her phone and her watch.

"Mr. Shaunessy sent me a layout of the building and the floors. The elevators are this way," Larry said.

Larry escorted everyone to their rooms on the top floor. There were only three floors and each door had a key taped to it.

"The regular doors will be in by the end of this month. Once those are here, we will replace your doors and keys," Larry said. "These are the only finished rooms in the hotel right now. They should all be complete by the end of next month."

Bailey's room was at the end of the hall. Just out in the hall was a window that overlooked the edge of the property and the Atlantic Ocean. It was breathtaking. She had to write that down in her notebook.

As she unpacked her things in her room, she felt a little tired. Sleep began to sound good to her when she realized she had been awake for over twenty-four hours. The room was just what she expected in a Hudson but with a little Irish flare in the wall décor.

While Bailey set up her laptop, she was glad she brought one of those adapters for the electrical outlet since it was different from what she used at home. The only problem was there was no internet.

Bailey brushed her teeth and changed her clothes before climbing into bed. Now was the best time for her to be in Ireland. She wouldn't be alone since she had her coworkers with her. Somehow, she would find time to research her book while secretly watching for the man who had haunted her dreams. She set the hotel clock and pulled the duvet over her shoulders.

"I'm here, Shaun. I finally made it to Ireland." She rolled over and closed her eyes, picturing the man she had seen every night for the past year. Then she heard his voice in her dream.

"Hello love. I can't wait to see you. Now that you're on Ireland time, I'll have to join you later."

A little disappointed, she smiled at the thought she was so close to finally meeting him. She fell asleep with Shaun on her mind.

Hours later, Bailey awoke refreshed and excited but very hungry. She freshened up and changed clothes into some jeans and a long-sleeved shirt. Remembering how chilly it was earlier this morning, she grabbed a jacket and put it on. She checked the clock in the room. It was 2 p.m. so she had a couple hours before meeting the new owner. She turned off the alarm, since she no longer needed it.

She glanced around the lobby and found a couple men still working on the wallpaper.

"Excuse me," she said.

Both men turned toward her.

"Can you tell me where I can find a restaurant within walking distance from here?"

"Yes, miss, it's just down the road a bit." He pointed in the direction the bus had come from earlier in the day.

"Thank you," she said. Bailey slipped the strap from her camera bag over her shoulder and headed out the lobby door.

She would get some exercise while she was here, since this hotel sat on a hill.

A year ago, she would never have ventured out on her own. But she was hungry and she had to get over her fear. Her fear of doing things alone was the one obstacle that kept her from actually enjoying her life.

Once she left the property, she realized there were no sidewalks. She walked along the edge of the road until she found a row of shops, sharing a sidewalk. All the shops had colorful doors, which made each of them stand out.

She read the names over the doors. Some were in Gaelic, and some had both Gaelic and English names.

She found O'Donnel's, which looked like a restaurant, and went inside. There weren't too many people inside at this time of day. Since the bar was the center of attraction, she sat at the bar. The place was light and airy, nothing like the pubs in her dreams where the lighting was low.

A good-looking young man approached her. "What'll you have, miss?"

She read the bartender's name. "Are you still serving lunch, Patrick?"

"Of course," he said. He handed her a menu. "Are you real hungry?"

"I'm starving," she said. She glanced over the menu, but couldn't help looking into the bartender's eyes. He had a beautiful smile and if she had to guess, he was the age of her oldest son.

"Then I would recommend a burger with chips. Really filling. Have you had one yet?"

"Not an Irish burger, but it sounds good. I'll try that and a beer."

"Which one?"

"Do you have an amber ale?"

"Why, yes. Would you prefer an American imported beer?"

"No. What's your favorite?"

"I'm partial to Smithwick's."

"Then that's what I'll have, Patrick." She handed him the menu.

"I'll be right back."

He was back in no time with the beer. After a few sips, Bailey glanced down the long end of the bar and noticed a couple of men sitting at the far end, carrying on a conversation. She nearly choked on her beer when she realized who the familiar, dark-haired man was. He had bits of gray running through his hair. His profile was handsome. Her pulse quickened at the thought that this man could be her dream lover. *Could she be that lucky?* This place did not resemble any of the pubs in her dreams although she had the same dream of meeting him over and over.

When she noticed he had glanced her way, she bit her bottom lip to hide her smile. Was he looking at her? Had she imagined his smile? No. He had looked at someone else. She would have to save her imagination for her book writing. Her life was not that exciting.

Moments later, the good-looking man spoke to Patrick,

then left. What if this was her only chance to meet him? Her heart pounded in her chest. No. She would not chase after a man. She had not done that in any of her dreams and she wouldn't do it now. Besides, what if he was married?

Glancing around the pub, she realized another couple had left their table. Before she could check her watch, Patrick set her plate before her.

"Wow, that's a lot of food," she said. She cut her burger in half. It was too big to handle, otherwise.

"So, what brings you to Ireland?" Patrick asked.

"Two things, Patrick. One, I'm part of a Hudson team that's here to help train people and open the new Hudson Inn down the street. And the other is doing research for my book." She didn't dare tell him the third reason.

"What kind of book?" he asked. He seemed genuinely interested.

"It's a romance."

"So you're an author, then?"

"Yes. I'm still new at this, but I've got a few books out already."

"Well, I'll be seeing more of you then, until you get the hotel kitchen up and running."

"How do you know about that?"

"My father is one of the owners."

Michael Shaunessy stopped by the church on his way back to his home in Roundstone. He was excited and had to share his news with someone.

"Father Ambrose," he said. He reached his hand out to the priest he had known since he 'crossed over'.

"Michael, what brings you here at this hour?" He directed Michael to the last row of seats in the back of the church.

"Business, Father. I'm searching for a location for Patrick's vetery and, well, a means to obtain funds for opening the clinic." He sat down and leaned an arm over the back of the pew.

"And have you had any luck?" Father asked.

"Findley offered to help with the fundraising banquet. He said he'd find a location in Limerick to hold the banquet. I've got a few more people to contact before I can set everything up." He glanced at his watch.

"Ah, and I bet Fionnuala will help as well."

Michael nodded. Fionnuala was the one person he didn't want to run into. But calling on Findley was a package deal. He sat up and crossed his arms over his chest. When Jack Findley was involved in something lucrative, his daughter Fionnuala wanted in on it. If Jack's wife hadn't inherited her family's pub, O'Malley's, then Fionnuala would be out of a job.

"Have you had more dreams, Michael?" Father asked, interrupting Michael's thoughts.

"Since we last talked, yes. But now I know they were not dreams, Father."

"No?"

"They were premonitions. I believe they will happen, just the way I described them to you."

"And how do you know this, Michael?"

"I saw her, Father. She's real and right here in Round-stone." Of course he didn't give Father Ambrose all the details. The most intimate moments he savored for himself. He didn't mention to Father Ambrose that his best friend and guardian angel, Kalen, had let him hear her prayers. She had cried out to God, through her pain, asking for the love she craved. A prayer he had prayed himself while married to Megan. Michael knew Bailey's pain and felt her anguish. He asked Kalen if he could answer Bailey's prayer.

In his past life, while he was still in spirit form, he and Kalen answered many prayers for God, if it was God's will. But one night, Kalen allowed him to hear Bailey's pleas and opened a connection between them through her guardian angel, Luke. Luke had been seeking a way to help her through her rough patches when he thought of Kalen. So now, Bailey had three angels on her side.

"So, how is your hotel coming along, Michael?" Father asked.

"I tried hiring staff online as well as using an advert with an article about the Hudson Inn opening up here in Roundstone. I'm hoping to get some interest this week. We want to get the hotel up and running from day one."

"Is it finished, then?"

"No. We have all the interior rooms to do. The outside is finished except for some landscaping. The wallpapering is taking the longest time, but we have to keep to Hudson standards as we go along."

"This is exciting, Michael. Having a hotel in Roundstone will open up the tourist trade," Father said.

"That's what I'm hoping for, Father."

After she finished eating at O'Donnel's, Bailey headed to the next little shop to see if she could buy a phone card and a battery for her watch. She had to be able to contact her daughter somehow before the hotel got internet. While she walked, she snapped some pictures.

After the shopkeeper replaced her watch battery, he

showed her how to use the phone card. Bailey called her daughter on her way back to the hotel. Everything was fine in the States and Bailey let her daughter know that she was fine in Ireland.

She got back to the hotel with a few minutes to spare and headed up to her room to grab her notebook and pen and put her camera bag up. By the time she returned to the lobby area, many of the workers were heading out the lobby entrance.

While she stood in the lobby, Linda, Maria and Ted joined her. Within minutes, Larry walked in through the front entrance.

The glare of the sun made it hard to see their faces, but she recognized Larry's shape, along with another one, who must be the other owner.

She opened her notebook, and put the date at the top. When she glanced up, a man in a dark blue suit stood before her. She slowly looked up the suit to his face and realized she stood before her dream lover she had called "Shaun".

REVELATIONS

Bailey's mouth dropped open and her eyes widened. Her pulse rate shot up just seeing him. This wasn't the way she was supposed to meet him. She never had a dream like this. It was always in a pub.

Before she could form a word, the Irishman offered his hand. She put her notebook and pen in her left hand and shook his hand. His hand was warm and strong.

"You must be Bailey," he said. He wrapped both his hands over hers.

"How did you know?"

He leaned close and whispered in her ear. "You've been in my dreams for over a year now."

"Oh, my gosh," she whispered back. He was so close. His masculine scent helped calm her. Was he wearing cologne? Did he always smell this nice?

"This is Michael Shaunessy, the other owner of the new Hudson Inn," Larry said. "Mr. Shaunessy has graciously invited us to an informal dinner at his residence." With that,

Mr. Shaunessy released her hand. She missed his warmth already.

He shook everyone's hand and personally greeted them as she watched. He seemed equally nice to everyone. She liked him.

The rest of the team gathered around.

"Is it far from here?" Ted asked.

"I'll be driving everyone there," Larry said.

"Oh, thank goodness," Linda said.

Larry ushered everyone outside to the parking lot. His rental was an SUV. Ted sat next to Larry in the front and Bailey, Linda, and Maria squeezed into the middle seats. The back of the SUV was more or less trunk space.

Linda leaned close to Bailey. "What did Mr. Shaunessy say to you?" she asked.

"Uh, he thought he recognized my name," she lied. How could she even speak about her dreams? "I'm an author and I have some books out." She only knew Linda for a little over a year, but not as well as the group of women she worked with at the Smoky Brewery in east Tennessee. She had worked at the Brewery before working at the Hudson and now she worked at both. She had shared some of her dreams with the women at the Brewery, but not all the details.

"I'm going to Ireland," she announced to her Brewery coworkers one day.

"Don't tell me you're going because of that dream?" Dee asked.

Bailey had raised an eyebrow. "Yes and no," she said.

"You write books?" Linda asked.

"Yes, in my spare time."

"What kind of books?" Maria asked.

"Romance." She hoped the conversation would stop. She hated lying, but the only lie was that Michael knew about her writing. He did recognize her but it was from the dreams and not her books.

"That's cool," Maria said.

"I'm starving," Linda said, bringing Bailey back to reality.

"Me, too," Maria added.

"I think we're all hungry," Larry said.

Bailey didn't say anything because she was glad she had eaten. This was going to be an interesting evening. Her pulse kicked up a notch when she thought of seeing him again. Did Mr. Shaunessy have the same erotic dreams she had? How could that even be? She had told Dee just a few things, but no one knew what was said or done in her dreams but her. But *he* had dreams of *her*.

The ride was short and they arrived at a beautiful house tucked back on a hill with a nice size driveway and parking area in back.

She followed behind the group and took in the architecture of the house. *If only she had her camera with her*. She had her notebook and pen still clutched in her hands. They all entered through a large patio area with lots of French doors. At one door, a man stood greeting the small group.

"Welcome, come in," a handsome gentleman said. When she got close enough, she recognized him.

"Hello, Patrick!"

He reached his hand out to her. "Why hello—"

"It's Bailey Jackson. How are you?" His hands were warm and firm.

"I'm fine, and you?"

"This is a gorgeous house."

"Why, thank you. My father designed it himself."

"I love his taste in design," she said.

"He would be happy to know that," Patrick said. He pulled the door closed behind her. "Our nights get a little chilly here in Roundstone."

"Ah, there you are," Mr. Shaunessy said, entering the room. "Help yourselves." He showed off a large counter with lots of finger foods.

"Can I get anyone a drink?" Patrick asked.

"This is my son, Patrick. He will soon be the new veterinarian in Roundstone but he's currently tending bar at O'Donnel's."

"Have you got any Smithwick's in the house?" Bailey asked.

"We're on the clock, Bailey," Linda said.

Bailey glanced at Larry then at Mr. Shaunessy.

"No, you're not on the clock. Eat what you want and drink what you want, provided we have it," Mr. Shaunessy said. He touched Bailey's shoulder. "But I would suggest a Guinness."

"Well, I guess I could try one," she said. She glanced at Patrick.

"Sure, sure. We have both on tap."

"On tap?" Ted headed straight to Patrick. "I'll take a Guinness, too, please."

Since Bailey wasn't very hungry, she picked up a small plate and put a few things on it so she wouldn't fill up on beer.

She watched her coworkers fill up their plates to overflowing. None of them had eaten since the flight.

"You know you have to wait for the foam to settle before

drinking a Guinness?" Mr. Shaunessy said.

"Really? And how long is that?"

"I'll let you know when it's ready," he said. Patrick set the drink down before her.

"So, what would you like us to call you?" Bailey asked.

"Michael is fine," he said.

"You sure you don't prefer Mr. Shaunessy?"

He leaned close in a whisper. "You can even call me Shaun, if you prefer."

Her mouth dropped open again and her heart pounded. *That's the name she had called him in her dreams because she didn't know his name.*

He lifted her chin up with his finger to close her mouth.

"You do that a lot, don't you?" he asked.

"You've surprised me a lot tonight."

"I hope in a good way." He had the sexiest smile she had ever seen.

"Yes. So far, it's been very good."

Larry came up to them and moved between her and Michael. He started talking to Michael about the hotel and she felt out of place. After her pounding heart had finally settled down, she turned and spoke to Linda and Maria.

"These are scrumptious," Linda said. "I need to get the recipe."

"Here you go," Patrick moved a paper toward her on the counter.

"What's this?" Bailey asked.

"These are my dad's favorite recipes for finger foods. He had me make copies for anyone who asked."

"Oh, I'd love a copy, too, please," Bailey said.

He handed her and Maria a page of recipes as well.

"You can drink your Guinness now," Patrick said.

"Mmm. It's delicious." She leaned a little closer to

Patrick. "Don't tell your father, but I like the Smithwick's more."

"It's our secret," he said.

"So, you're going to be a vet?" Maria asked.

"Technically, I am a vet. I'm saving up money for the clinic right now."

"My daughter is a vet tech in the States," Bailey said.

"Really? I'm going to need one of those myself. Did she go to school for that?"

"No, she had on-the-job training. Many of the girls who did go to school for it quit when they found out how hard the work was. They all thought it was just office work."

"Oh, it's assisting in surgeries and doing a lot more for the animals," he explained.

"Yes. She's learned a lot since she started working there. She loves it, but it is hard work. Tell me, Patrick, will you be seeing small animals or large farm animals?"

"Both."

"Have you got a name for your clinic?" Linda asked.

"All Creatures Great and Small," he said.

"Oh, I love that!" Bailey said. "It's perfect."

Michael moved toward the three of them. "What's perfect?" he asked.

"The name Patrick chose for his clinic. I love it."

She suddenly started hearing some music playing in the background. "That's pretty," she said.

"Irish music," Patrick said. "It was too quiet in here."

"Since I have everyone's attention," Michael started. "I wanted to let you know the computers and desks should arrive tomorrow and we'll have internet by the end of the day."

"That's wonderful," Larry said. "Have you gotten any responses from the ads?"

"Yes. I'll be interviewing people tomorrow and later this week."

"Great. We can start the training by the following week," Larry said.

"In the meantime, what do we do for food?" Ted asked.

"Is O'Donnel's the only restaurant in town?" Maria asked. "I noticed it's quite a ways from the hotel."

"I'll take care of breakfast for the next few days," Michael said. "We should have the kitchen up and running by later this week, so we can stock up on food to get us through the next few weeks."

"That sounds like a plan," Larry said.

Larry appeared to be ready to leave.

"Is there anything I can help you with as far as cleaning up?" Bailey offered.

"Why thank you, Bailey. I'm sure I can find something for you to do. I'll be glad to run her back to the hotel if you're in a hurry to leave," Michael said to Larry.

"That will work. Everyone else ready to go?" Larry asked.

Just as quickly, everyone rushed to the back door to leave.

How odd, Bailey thought. After Michael was so gracious to feed them, no one else volunteered to help clean up.

She rolled up her sleeves and started stacking the dishes next to the sink.

Patrick had left the room and when he came back, everyone was gone but Bailey.

"What happened?" he asked.

"I think Larry was in a hurry to get back to the hotel."

"What about the others?"

"I think they didn't want to get stuck cleaning up since we aren't on the clock."

"Did Dad walk them out?"

"Yes. Tell me, is any of this food salvageable for another day?"

"The sandwiches and the bacon dogs. Everything else we'll toss."

"Where are your containers to put them in?" she asked.

Patrick retrieved a couple containers while Bailey ran the water for the dishes.

Michael walked back in to the kitchen. "I can tell a lot about the character of your coworkers from their behavior tonight," Michael said.

"Really?" she asked.

"Yes. No one else volunteered and that tells me they won't do more than what is required of them."

"I hope you have better luck with your interviews this week, Dad."

"Me, too. You'll have to think about that as well when you hire for your clinic, son."

Bailey was finished with the dishes in no time. She hadn't thought about her coworkers in that light before, but when she thought about their past actions at their own hotel, she realized when it was quitting time, they left. She had always made sure she didn't leave anything undone before heading home. But she had always been that way.

After wiping down the counters, Bailey put up the towel.

"Is there anything else I can help you with, Michael?"

"I think we got it, Bailey. And thank you, Patrick, for all your hard work."

"Any time, Dad. I'll see you in the morning. Good night, Dad. Good night, Bailey."

"Good night, Patrick. The food was delicious."

She watched him head up the stairs, then awkwardly glanced around. "I don't think I brought anything with me except my notebook, pen, and room key," she said. She picked up her things that had been on a stool.

"Come with me." Michael took her hand and led her into a large living area with a beautiful fireplace. They sat down on the sofa, beside each other, near the fire.

"I had no idea you would be part of the Hudson team, Bailey, but I had looked forward to meeting you so many different ways."

"Me, too." Bailey fidgeted with her key and felt her face grow hot. Here she sat, next to the man who had seen her naked in all her dreams, and wondered if he had the same exact dreams.

"I have to explain something to you." We have been sharing dreams each night because I heard your prayer to your guardian angel."

"My angel? How?" She thought back to the night she cried out for God to help her find the love she craved. Her husband didn't show her the affection she wanted and he certainly didn't act like he cared for her anymore. Her heart raced, thinking of the night she had asked her angel for his help.

"My guardian angel, Kalen, opened up communications between your guardian angel, Luke, and me." He held both her hands and ran his thumbs across the tops of them, caressing her skin. His touch sent an electric tingle throughout her body.

"Bailey, at one time I was an angel. Kalen and I would answer prayers through people's dreams. I fell in love with this beautiful woman, Megan. I crossed over from an angel to human, but discovered too late that she didn't love me the way I loved her. We had Patrick, who is a beautiful soul, with a gift for healing animals. Megan died a couple years ago from cancer. It was after that we met in your dreams."

Bailey's heart pounded now. She'd been sharing her dreams with an angel? Erotic dreams at that. Her face heated even more at the thought. "The dreams seemed so real to me. I looked forward to them each night. I wouldn't have made it through my last year of marriage if I didn't have my dreams to look forward to."

"Believe me, Bailey, they were real." He lifted her chin and kissed her sweetly on the lips. It was the kiss she had waited a lifetime for. Her arms were around his neck. His arms were around her waist and back. It grew more intense and passionate. She could feel the passion rising within her and her nervousness left. She didn't want it to stop, but she had to come up for air.

"What happens now?" She leaned her forehead against his. "Do we pretend this never happened?" she asked.

"I'd like to see you every night, Bailey, like in our dreams, only I want to touch you and hold you, kissing you in the flesh."

She wanted that too. Was that asking too much? "Do we keep our relationship a secret from the others?"

"For now, I think that's wise."

"Since you were honest with me, I need to be honest with you," Bailey said.

"Go on."

"In the dreams, I didn't have any inhibitions. But in reality, I'm really not that assertive. I'm more reserved than that."

"We'll take it one step at a time." Michael stood and held his hand out to her.

Bailey took his hand and he led her to his bedroom.

Inside, Bailey's heart pounded again. What was she thinking? What was she doing? This was not her reality. Sure, she wrote about people going about relationships this way, but it was someone else.

Michael turned on the light. The large bed was the center of the room, with wraparound windows on either side. On the side where they entered, there was a chaise lounge to the left and behind it, a bathroom. On the other side of the bedroom door was a large walk-in closet.

"I really love your house." Her heart rate went down a notch. She felt a little more at ease now.

"Let me show you the bathroom," he said. He took her hand and walked her to the door.

When she walked inside, it was roomy with the largest tub she had ever seen. It had a separate shower across from it, and two sinks, and a toilet.

"This tub looks big enough for two," she said.

"'Tis. I had hoped to use it with Megan but she never would share it with me."

"It looks like all you need is some bubble bath."

"I do have that," he added.

Bailey set the plug and ran the water, trying to get the temperature just right. "I like a hot bath. How about you?" she asked.

Michael lifted her chin and kissed her tenderly. She wrapped her arms around his neck, rising on her toes, and returned the kiss. This was more like how her dreams started. His kiss started her passions rising. She enjoyed kissing Michael. Her husband didn't like kissing that much, but he waited years before telling her that. She had thought it was something she had done to deserve the scowl he gave her each time she asked for a kiss.

Her passion built up inside her the longer he kissed her. Then she felt Michael's warm flesh against hers, his hands roaming up and down her back.

"How did we get naked?"

"I still have the power where I can blink clothes on or off," he said.

"Well, before you take me back to the hotel, you need to blink them back on."

"Sure, sure." He reached for the bubble bath that sat on a shelf above the side of the tub and poured it into the water.

Bailey stroked his back and realized he was well built for an older man. She began to feel comfortable around him.

After he finished pouring in the liquid bubbles, he caressed her back. She placed her hand on his chest, slowly caressing the black hairs that covered it. Her husband hadn't had hair on his chest. Michael pulled her into another kiss and she let her passions loose.

When the water reached the right level, Michael helped her step into the tub. Then he joined her.

THE FIRST NIGHT

"Ah, this is so warm. I love it. Thank you, Michael."

Michael joined Bailey in the warm bath, while the bubbles floated on the water. Taking a bubble bath used to be a luxury for her when she was married, but since her husband died, she managed to do it at least twice a week and shower all the other times when she was in a hurry.

She grabbed a washcloth and turned her back toward him. "Could you please wash my back?" She handed him the cloth and lifted her hair off her shoulders.

Michael took the cloth and ran it over her soft skin. He savored the feel of it, running his bare hand over her skin after cleansing it with the bubble bath. Slowly, he went down her back and then her shoulders. He realized she had backed up between his legs. He leaned forward, kissing her neck. Then he reached over her shoulder and ran the washcloth over her breasts. She moved back into him, arousing him more with her nearness. He moved his hands with the washcloth, over her belly and down to her core. She spread her legs for him, and he began using his fingers to arouse her.

Megan had refused to bathe with him, no matter how hard he tried. It was always his fantasy to do this with Megan, but he was glad it was Bailey instead. She was moaning in pleasure now. She propped up her legs and he reached one hand to run the washcloth over one leg. Then switched hands to clean the other leg.

She turned toward him on her knees and kissed him, putting her hands around his neck. Then she straddled him, and taking the washcloth, she washed his chest, then his shoulders and arms. Then getting on her knees again, she leaned over his body, washing his back.

He took her breast into his mouth and suckled it, wrapping his arms around her ass.

"Hmm. Don't forget the other one," she said.

He did as he was told, enjoying every minute of this foreplay, while she continued to wash his back.

Once he was done, she began to wash his lad. He thought he would lose control. She spent a lot of time moving up and down his shaft with her hands. Then, when he thought she was done, she pulled him forward, planting herself on his lad, wrapping her legs around him.

She leaned back and he started his rhythm moving slowly at first, then faster and faster until he exploded inside her.

She moved close to him, holding him tight. "I've always wanted to do this," she said.

"This was my fantasy, too," he said. He held her in his arms, caressing her back. He couldn't get enough of her soft skin. He didn't want this time to end, but the water was getting cold.

She slowly stood in the tub and reached for a towel. She helped him up and slowly dried him off all over. Then she handed him the towel and he returned the favor, only he took more time to wipe her dry, enjoying the feel of her skin under the towel. He stopped to kiss her neck and realized she really loved that.

By the time he got out of the tub, he was hard again. He drained the water and blinked some clothes onto the chair near the tub.

"Are these for me?" she asked.

"Yes. I wanted to watch you dress."

"And what about you?" She picked up the soft pink gown. It was a nightgown.

He wrapped a towel around himself. "We aren't finished yet."

"No?"

"No." He took her hand and walked her toward the bed.

Bailey pulled the covers back.

He tossed his wet towel on the floor and climbed into the bed. This night was turning out better than he thought.

She crawled into bed, curling up next to him. He wrapped his arm around her.

"Am I staying here all night?"

"Would you? I'd love to wake up beside you in the morning."

She kissed him good night and curled up with him again.

Her back was toward him, and he pulled her close. Having Bailey in his arms made him happy. He didn't want to think about how life was without her.

"Thank you, Michael," she said.

"For what?"

"For tonight and for letting me live out a fantasy."

He kissed the top of her head. "I love being part of your fantasy. Thank you, Bailey," he said.

"For what?"

"Thank you for coming to Ireland and letting me live out my greatest fantasy."

She turned toward him and took his face in her hands, kissing him sweetly on the lips. He returned her kiss, deepening it. He pulled her closer and wrapped his leg over her hips. She held him tight, arousing him all over again.

"My lad has not had this much action in years, Bailey."

"Do you want me to stop kissing you?"

"No!"

She started with his neck and moved down his chest, kissing and licking him all over. Never had he gotten this kind of attention from Megan. It was all he could do to get her to kiss him each morning or at night. Occasionally, he stopped Bailey to kiss her lips. She had kissable lips and he loved that about her. When she got to his belly, he took over and kissed her the same way, from neck to belly and then finished the job with the two of them climaxing at the same time.

"You're wearing me out, Bailey Jackson," he said.

"As long as you're enjoying it, don't complain."

"I'll never complain, just stating a fact."

Bailey slept well, re-living her conversation with her coworkers at the Brewery.

After she had told Dee that she was going to Ireland, and Dee asked if it was about her dream, Crystal asked, "What dream?" Crystal, one of the servers, had approached the Hostess stand with a stack of menus.

"She had a dream about meeting a sexy Irishman in a pub," Dee said.

Bailey had taken the menus from Crystal and stacked them up in the box on the side of the Hostess stand.

"Nuh uh," Crystal said. *"Was that before or after your husband died?"*

"Actually, the dream started before he died." She crossed her arms over her chest. *"I'm going there to do research for my latest book I'm writing."*

"And what about the dream lover?" Tammy asked. Her eyebrows raised. Tammy was another hostess and she had a big smile on her face.

"Well, if he exists, then I hope I meet him while I'm there," she said.

"And what if he doesn't exist?" Dee asked.

"It's worth a try. The dream was too real to ignore. Anyway, I'm going to have fun while I'm there and I'm not leaving Ireland until I'm kissed by an Irishman."

David, the manager walked up to the Hostess stand. *"Who's kissing who?"* he asked, his dark eyebrows raised.

"She's not leaving Ireland until she's kissed by an Irishman," Dee explained as she walked off to her table.

"Hey, ya'll get to work or look busy," he said. He waved his hands like he was shooing flies.

Tammy took the towel and a sanitizer bottle and wiped down tables. Crystal went back to her table. And Bailey was left with her thoughts.

And now, she lay in the arms of her dream lover and he was everything she had imagined and more. Although she didn't have a dream like what happened this evening, she had fantasized about sharing a bath with Michael. And now, she could say she was thoroughly kissed by an Irishman.

Hours later, an alarm went off. She turned toward Michael.

"What's that noise?"

Michael rubbed his face. "Ah, you're still here, love."

"Of course I am."

He pulled her into a hug and a kiss, wrapping a leg over her hips. "That's my alarm on my watch. I'll have to pick up some sweet rolls at the bakery as soon as they open this morning."

"And what are you going to do about me?"

"I'll just tell everyone I picked you up early to help me."

Bailey climbed out of bed and headed into the bathroom. After taking care of business, she approached Michael. "Okay, what are we going to do about my clothes?"

Michael blinked and she was dressed in a floral print dress with a light jean jacket and dressy sandals.

"I love it! Can I keep these?"

"Of course, love. Now I need to take care of business and I'll see you shortly."

Bailey found her way back into the kitchen, but Patrick was already there.

"Good morning, Patrick."

"Oh, hello, Bailey. I didn't know you were here. I'm making coffee if you'd like some."

"Oh, yes, please. Is there anything I can help you with?"

"Well, that depends on what you want to eat."

"Your father said he had to pick up some sweet rolls from the bakery when they opened."

"Ah, Patrick. You beat me to the coffee," Michael said.

"I'm off today, Dad. I thought I'd work on my website."

"Be a good man and drop off those leftover finger foods this afternoon."

"Sure, dad, but do you think that will be enough?"

"You're right. I'll order something from O'Donnel's and pick it up."

"Are you ready, Bailey?" Michael asked.

"Yes, I am. Thanks for the great coffee, Patrick."

"My pleasure."

Michael ushered Bailey out the side door to the patio and parking area.

"I found this on the coffee table," Michael said. He handed her a key.

"Oh, my. I couldn't get into my room without this. Thanks, Michael." She slipped the key into her jacket pocket. "By the way, what happened to my clothes that you blinked off?"

"They are at my house. I can blink them off, I can't make them disappear."

"Good to know. Thanks. I'll get them later."

Within minutes, they were at the bakery.

"It smells so good in here," Bailey said.

"Wait 'til you taste their rolls," Michael said.

He placed the order and then ordered a different variety for the next day. Michael carried the sweet rolls and Bailey carried the drink holders to the car.

"Just for safety, we'll put everything on the floor in the back," Michael said.

"Good idea. I wouldn't want to wear the coffee in this nice dress."

As they drove off, Bailey had a thought. "I know we will be keeping this relationship private from the rest of the group, but what about Patrick? Don't you think he should know?"

"Absolutely. I'll tell him tonight."

"I like Patrick. He reminds me of my oldest son. I'd like to help him somehow with his project."

Michael glanced at Bailey. "That's very thoughtful of

you, Bailey."

"I like animals and what he is doing is important. I'll come up with an idea and let you know."

Michael pulled up into the Hudson parking lot. The workers were busy with the landscaping.

Michael gathered the rolls and Bailey carried the coffees into the lobby.

"Hmm. Let me see if they've started on our training room," Michael said.

Bailey glanced around the lobby. The workers were putting up the finishing touches on the wallpaper trim.

"We've got a table," Michael called out from a side room.

Bailey headed to the room. There were two men setting up tables on one end of the room.

Michael had set the rolls out and Bailey set the coffee next to the rolls. While Michael texted Larry, she set up the creamers and other condiments.

Another man came in with a cart full of computers. The three men began opening boxes and putting computers together.

"We'll need a couple more tables," Michael said.

Within a few minutes, Linda, Maria, Ted and Larry came into the room. They enjoyed their rolls and coffee so much, there was nothing left.

Bailey started cleaning up the area. She put all the trash into the bag that had contained the rolls. She found a large bag for the trash. And was able to wipe down the tables.

"I have a few interviews this morning," Michael said to Larry. "Just make sure the computers are set up properly for the training."

"Will do."

Bailey made her way to the kitchen. She wanted to see if there was a trash can inside. Instead, she found two men unloading refrigerators. She went and found Larry and he took care of the kitchen.

When Bailey got back to the training room, Linda was chatting with Maria.

"I think they are setting up your kitchen today, Linda. Maybe we can cook something tomorrow."

"Tomorrow? I thought it would be later this week."

"Well, I guess they are ahead of schedule. It's better than eating out every night, don't you think?"

"I kind of like not having to cook," Linda said.

"Really? Then why did you come to Ireland?"

"I just wanted to get away, you know, like having a vacation."

"Well, we're supposed to be working. We just get some fringe benefits while we are here," Bailey said. She thought about her benefits from last night and smiled.

"The problem with that is we are stuck here at the hotel," Maria said.

"The shops are within walking distance from here," Bailey said.

"There are no sidewalks," Linda said.

"Well, if you like being stuck here, then you're welcome to stay. If I need something, I'm going to walk to town and get it," Bailey said. She glanced at her watch. It was late morning and the men were still setting up the computers. One man approached them.

"I need to speak with one of the owners," the man said.

"Come with me. I think I know where one of them is." Bailey stood and ushered the man to the kitchen. Sure enough, Larry was inside while some men were installing the oven.

"Larry, this gentleman needs to speak to an owner," she said.

Larry came toward them and started talking to the man. She waited until they were finished. "Larry, is there anything you need me to do?" Bailey asked.

"Not at the moment."

"Okay. You have my number, right?"

"Yes."

"Call me if you need anything. I'll be upstairs for a few minutes."

She headed to her room. She hadn't been there since yesterday. She needed to phone her daughter and let her know she was all right. Her daughter worried a lot so she tried to contact her every couple of days.

After she got off the phone with her daughter, she realized she had left her notebook and pen at Michael's, along with the recipes Patrick gave her. She would have to remember to get them later. She searched through her things to see if she had another notebook, but she didn't.

All her notes about Ireland were in her notebook, along with the characterizations she had done earlier. Her premise for the story was in there as well. She was eager to do some writing while she had time, but she needed her notebook for that.

If she had some free time this afternoon, she would head to town and see if she could find a notebook or journal. How could she come to Ireland with just one notebook? A writer needs to be prepared. She pulled her camera out and charged the battery. As she searched through her camera bag for any scrap of paper, her phone rang. It was an Irish phone number.

Michael headed to his appointments in Limerick. He wanted to find quality people to work at his Hudson Inn, but would they be willing to drive to Roundstone?

Since he had to meet Fionnuala, he set the appointments in Limerick to save him driving time. While he drove, he thought about the time he spent with Bailey. She was as he had imagined. Her soft, flowing brown hair, sparkling brown eyes, and beautiful smile, made his heart happy. He couldn't wait to see her again. And the bubble bath he shared with her was perfect.

He had to figure a more discreet way of taking her home with him so as to not arouse suspicion with the other team members. He didn't want to embarrass her.

He also had to remember to speak to Patrick about his relationship with Bailey. Patrick would understand.

Finally, Michael pulled into the parking lot at another Hudson property in Limerick. He had rented the meeting room to conduct his interviews and then meet with Fionnuala and Mr. Daly, who was in advertising, about Patrick's fundraising banquet. Once that was settled, he could finish with the opening of the Hudson Inn before starting on Patrick's clinic.

His appointments went well. He had a few candidates for General Manager. He wanted to have his General Manager do some of the heavy interviewing to free him up to check on the construction renovations and other things he needed to do to finish the project.

He grabbed a sandwich in the hotel's restaurant before facing his last appointment. He didn't trust being alone with Fionnuala at all. His thoughts went back to the day, shortly after Megan's death, when he had been sitting in his favorite pub, drowning his sorrow with ale. Jack and Fionnuala had stopped by to see him, only Jack left a while later. He and Fionnuala…well, he didn't know what they had done. All he remembered was waking up the next morning in a hotel room with her.

That brought his thoughts to Father Ambrose. After confessing what he thought had happened with Fionnuala, he also confessed his first dream about Bailey. He never told Father Ambrose that he could communicate with his own guardian angel, or that Kalen told him what her guardian angel had said. He didn't even tell the priest that he could put himself into someone's dream and manipulate the dream somewhat. Until Bailey arrived in Ireland, his dreams were only dreams.

"I wouldn't be getting my hopes up if I were you, Michael. You dream of a love that not many married people actually have. Of all the couples I've spoken to over the years, so many are resigned to loving someone who doesn't return the love they expected. Only a handful of those happily married couples are experiencing the love that you long for," Father Ambrose had said.

He remembered seeing the age in Father's eyes. Although Father Ambrose appeared older than himself, Father had not seen the love between humans that he had seen over the centuries. That love was out there, but like Father said, so many were resigned to live without it. If he had listened to Kalen years ago before crossing over, he would have learned that Megan was not his soul mate. But she had been beautiful and he had been drawn to her beauty. The years they had together were good, but the love he had seen between soul mates had not been there. Was it so wrong to ask for a second chance at love? Others had gotten second chances, why couldn't he? Was he willing to risk his heart once more, only to be disappointed?

4

CALM BEFORE THE STORM

"Hello?" Bailey said.

"Hello, is this Bailey Jackson?" a male voice asked.

"Yes, who is this?"

"It's Patrick Shaunessy, Bailey. My dad had everyone's phone number listed on the fridge. I found your journal on the coffee table this morning."

"Oh, thank you, Patrick! I wondered where I had left it."

"I thought you might be needing it. I hope you don't mind, but I looked through it for a name. When I saw the characters you wrote about, I thought it might be yours, but then I found your name in the front with your number."

"Oh, yes. I do that in case I lose it."

"I can ride my bike over to the hotel and bring it to you, if you like?"

"That's sweet of you, Patrick. I think I'll be seeing your dad later since he's bringing us dinner. I can get it from him to save you a trip."

"Well I don't think Dad is stopping by the house before bringing dinner to everyone. Besides, I'd like to see how the hotel is coming along."

"Well, if you insist, I'll be here all day. If you can't find me in the lobby area, I'll be in the meeting room."

"See you in a bit," he said.

When Bailey ended the call, she realized the premise of her story was about her dream lover and finding a second chance at love. Would Patrick figure out it was about her and Michael?

Bailey saved Patrick's number in her phone and headed downstairs.

She glanced into the meeting room. Larry was there, along with some technicians, working on wiring something.

"How's it going, Larry? Anything you need me to do?" Bailey asked.

"Not yet. The real work will start soon enough. I expect everyone to be here bright and early to help me get these computers set up for training," he said. He glanced at his watch. "I need to check something in the kitchen." Larry left the meeting room.

Bailey walked around the spacious lobby. Workers brought in cabinets for the other rooms. She also watched as a few others worked on a fireplace in the center of the lobby.

"Wow, this place is really coming along," Patrick said. He walked his bicycle into the lobby and parked it.

"Yes. I can't wait to see what the front desk will look like," she said.

"Is that your specialty?"

"Yes."

Patrick shrugged off a backpack and opened it.

"Did you want a tour? I can show you my room so you'll know what the finished rooms will look like."

"I'd love that," he said. He handed her the notebook and pen.

"Of course, this is the lobby. I'm not sure where the front desk will go, but there will be tables and chairs set up for breakfast and maybe by the fireplace, a small sofa or two for more intimate conversations," she said.

Patrick looked around, taking in the work being done.

"Over there will be our kitchen," she pointed. She headed in that direction. "We just got our appliances today." She opened the door and they peeked inside. There were a couple men setting up a freezer and Larry was there, telling them where to put it.

"This is nice," he said.

She headed out the door and led Patrick to the elevator area. Off to the side of the elevators were the restrooms. "Here are our toilets," she said. She used the term the Irish used for restrooms. Of course they would have 'toilets' written on the doors with the traditional male and female icons.

Patrick peeked inside. "Just like ours," he said.

"Now, at the end of this hall, they are putting in the pool," she said.

"An indoor pool?"

"Yes. I haven't seen it yet, but I was told they would have one."

They walked to the end and there was a glass door opening out to a small patio that surrounded one end of the pool. There were more toilets near the patio end. Men were inside the pool finishing the tile work. On the far end of the pool was another patio and door exiting to the parking lot.

"I can only show you my room, but they're bringing in cabinets today for the other unfinished rooms," she said.

Bailey and Patrick went back toward the elevators and

peeked in one of the unfinished rooms, where the workers were setting cabinets in the bathrooms.

"My room is upstairs," she said. When they got to her room, she unlocked the door and opened it. Patrick stepped inside.

She set the notebook near her computer. "I can't wait until we get internet. I can finally email my daughter and sons."

"This room is nice. Each room has its own toilet and tub?"

"Yes. Don't all hotels have that?"

"I'm not sure, but some of the bed and breakfasts don't. You share a toilet and tub with strangers."

"I don't think I'd like that," she said.

"Tell me, Bailey, is this story you're working on about my dad?"

"What makes you think that?" Her heart pounded. She had the feeling that Michael didn't talk to Patrick about their relationship.

"Did my dad tell you about his past?"

"A little, but I didn't meet him until after I wrote my characters."

"One of the characters sounds a lot like my dad, while another sounds like you."

"Well, writers do tend to use personal experience and familiar people to put in their stories." She hoped that would answer his questions.

"How long have you known my dad?"

"We just met the other day when he invited us to your place for a light dinner," she said.

"Somehow, I get the feeling you two have known each other longer than a couple days."

❧

While Michael looked over the applications of the General Manager candidates, Fionnuala and Mr. Daly walked into the room.

"Hello Michael. And how are you doing this fine day?" Fionnuala asked.

"Fine, fine, thanks for asking." He shook hands with her and Mr. Daly. "Have a seat," he said.

Before he could start his conversation about the fundraiser, he heard Bailey's voice in his head.

"Oh, Michael! Patrick has figured us out."

Bailey bit her bottom lip. She didn't want to lie to Patrick. He had only been kind to her. She had to tell him something.

"Let me rephrase that," Patrick said. "How well do you and my dad know each other?"

Bailey's face grew hot. "You're right, Patrick. Michael and I have had a spiritual connection that goes back at least a year."

"Spiritual connection?" Patrick asked.

"I don't know how else to explain it," she said.

"Do you mean you've had dreams with him in it, like in your story?"

Bailey closed her eyes and took a deep breath. When she opened them, Patrick was staring at her, waiting for an answer.

"I was married to a verbally abusive man for over twenty-six years. I cried myself to sleep many nights because of things he had said to me. One night, I remember praying to my guardian angel for help. It was afterward that I started having dreams of a nice man, who I would meet in different places in Ireland, but it was always the same dream. We met, we kissed, and we made love. That was it. But it got me through some really bad times in the last part of my marriage. My husband died last year of a heart attack."

Patrick rubbed his face. "So, you came to Ireland to find this dream lover?" he asked.

"I came as a team member to help train new people for his hotel. I also came to do research for this book, but I was *hoping* to see if my dreams were real. I clearly saw his face in my dreams. And when I met your father, I was surprised to see that he was actually real."

"This is a lot to take in right now," Patrick said.

"Yes, it is. I'm still trying to process this myself."

"I think I'll be going." Patrick walked to the door.

"Patrick?"

"Yes?"

"I really like you and your dad. And I really do want to help you with your new clinic, if you'll let me."

He nodded and then left the room.

Bailey closed her eyes and offered up a prayer. "Oh, Lord, please help me make this right for both of them."

After the meeting with Fionnuala and Mr. Daly, Michael felt better about the fundraiser. He would have to remember to always have another person at the meeting so she would not intimidate him. It seemed hard to say no to her when he was alone. He tried hard not to be in that situation after his last experience with her. He didn't trust Fionnuala at all.

Michael glanced at the clock in his car and realized he had a little time before picking up the food at O'Donnel's. He decided to go home and change into something more casual than a suit.

When he got inside the house, Patrick was in the kitchen, cooking a meal.

"Hello, son. How was your day?"

Patrick looked up from the stove and glanced at him. "I had a nice chat with Bailey today."

"Oh? What about?"

"Have you put yourself into her dreams, dad?"

"I helped answer her prayers, Patrick, and she answered mine."

Patrick poured the food from the pan onto his dish, then set the pan back on the stove. He turned off the burner. He rubbed his forehead.

"What's wrong?" Michael asked.

"What's wrong? You bring a woman you barely know into your home, acting like you've known each other for years, and ask me what's wrong? You know what's wrong, here, Dad. You penetrated her dreams and put yourself in them. You've been doing that for a year? Why?"

"She cried out for help. Out of loneliness and despair, she asked her guardian angel for help."

"Did you plant that thought in her head, too?"

"No. I… Kalen showed me her situation when he was contacted. Her guardian angel, Luke, opened up a connection between us. She was lonely and so was I. We both had married people who didn't love us as much as we loved them. Both of us felt an emptiness in our relationships. But she fascinated me, so I returned, night after night for over a year. It was her decision to come to Ireland. The spiritual connection is real because we are soul mates."

Patrick lowered his head and walked around the counter to face Michael, then hugged him. "I'm sorry, Dad. I want you to be happy. This was just so sudden."

Michael pulled back. "I would have told you sooner if I

knew she was coming to Ireland. I just learned she was here the other day."

"I wish you all the luck in the world, Dad. You deserve to be happy."

"Thank you, Patrick. I feel happy just being around her."

Michael quickly changed clothes and headed to O'Donnel's to pick up the food for the team members. On the way to the hotel, he called his candidate for General Manager. He wanted him to deal with his new employees and their training. The team members from the States would help in their transitioning and setting up the actual equipment and job descriptions. He had enough to deal with the renovations and to make sure everything was in place for those workers to finish the hotel.

When he pulled up to the entrance, Larry greeted him at the door. He handed Larry one of the bags of food.

"Is everything set up in the meeting room?" he asked. He and Larry walked through the lobby.

"Yes. We're all set to go over the computers tomorrow and make sure the program is running on all of them. I'll get everyone logged in so that we can test it. Once I know who the new employees are, I can set them up in the system for training." Larry set the bag on the only free table in the room.

"Brilliant. I've hired the new General Manager. He should be here sometime tomorrow. He's eager to start." Michael set his bag beside Larry's bag.

"Has he managed a hotel before?" Larry asked.

"Yes. He's been with Hudson properties in other cities in Ireland. I checked his credentials and references."

"Our tech guy showed up today and has been testing the

software on all the computers. He will be here until everyone finishes training and also, if the General Manager needs him to stay on after the opening, he can do that as well," Larry said.

"Brilliant," Michael said.

Larry pulled out his phone and sent everyone a text.

Michael set out the drinks and then sandwiches.

"I have an account at the local grocery store. If you want to take Linda with you and pick out some food for meals the rest of the week, you will have more options to choose from."

"How soon can we go?" Larry asked.

"You can go this evening and have something different for breakfast tomorrow," Michael said.

"Excellent."

Linda, Maria and Bailey walked into the room, followed by Ted.

"While you are eating, I want you all to think about what you want to eat the rest of this week and we'll make a list. Linda and I will go shopping tonight and we'll all take turns cooking the evening meals," Larry said.

"Does that mean I'm cooking breakfast every day?" Linda asked.

"Yes. That's what I'm paying you for, Linda. Tomorrow starts your workweek. Vacation time is over for everyone."

"I have some equipment and utensils I can bring back for you tonight. You can use them until your equipment comes in," Michael said.

Everyone helped themselves to the sandwiches and drinks, then found seats at the table. He noticed the women sat together, but Bailey was on the side he chose to sit. Ted sat with him and Larry.

"I can help you with breakfast, if you want, Linda, until I have a desk to work from," he heard Bailey say.

"I appreciate that. It's not so much the cooking, it's also the cleanup afterward," Linda said.

He turned to Larry. "Is there anything else I need to know about?" Michael asked.

"The kitchen is ready to stock. The bathroom cabinets are in place in all the rooms, and the pool is coming along slowly," Larry said.

"The toilets, tubs, and plumbers should be here tomorrow," Michael said.

"Wonderful. Everything is moving along a little faster than I expected," Larry said.

"It will take a while to get all of that in place, Larry, but I hope we continue to stay ahead."

After they finished eating, Bailey grabbed some paper from one of the printers and they started their list for meals.

"Where is the tech guy you spoke about?" Michael asked.

"He's staying in Limerick for now," Larry said.

"I'm sure Ted won't mind sharing a room with him until we can get another one ready for him?" Michael said.

Ted choked on his drink. "Uh, sure. Why not? How soon will he be staying here?" Ted asked.

Larry punched some numbers on his phone and stepped into the hall.

"I guess, we'll find out." Michael said.

"Oh, Ted," Bailey began. "What meal did you want to cook for us?"

"I don't cook."

"Well, we are all taking turns cooking, so what will you be fixing?" Linda said.

"Yes, we need to get the food and seasonings," Bailey said.

"Like I said, I don't cook."

"I suggest you try cooking something if everyone is taking turns," Michael said.

"Uh, I can make peanut butter and jelly sandwiches," Ted said.

Bailey leaned close to Linda and whispered.

"Okay, Ted. You will be making lunches for us every day since you don't cook. I'll pick out the jelly myself," Linda said.

"And everyone who cooks must clean up their own messes and the kitchen," Bailey added.

"That's not my job description," Ted said.

"We can fix that for you, Ted," Larry said. He walked up to the table, arms crossed. "Did you forget what Hudsonality is all about?"

Ted glanced at Larry and then Michael. "I guess I need a refresher."

"Maybe we can all use one when the new people have to sit through the video. It certainly wouldn't hurt," Bailey added.

"Brilliant!" Michael said. He patted her on the back. He caught Bailey biting her bottom lip. She was cute when she did that.

"It looks like Dave, our tech guy, will be joining us tomorrow and staying with Ted until Michael can get a room finished for him," Larry announced. "How's that list coming?"

"Almost finished," Linda said. "Will you two be doing any cooking?" she glanced at Larry and then Michael.

"I'll be glad to cook some burgers one night," Michael volunteered. He glanced at Larry.

Larry coughed. "I guess I can make something with chicken."

"I've added some side dishes we can heat up in the oven to save time," Linda said.

"Oh, I forgot to mention there will be a patio outside the pool area with a couple of grills. We can also use those for cooking," Michael added.

"I think I have my list completed," Linda announced.

Michael reached into his back pocket and pulled out his wallet. "Here's my card," he said. He handed it to Larry. "It's the hotel account."

"You ready, Linda?" Larry said.

She stood and walked out with Larry.

"I guess I better clean up my room," Ted said. He stood to leave.

"Well, I need someone to help me collect and bring over the utensils and pans we need for the meals," Michael said.

"Me!" Maria shouted.

"I'll be glad to help as well," Bailey said. She quickly cleaned up the mess in the meeting room and tossed the trash in the bag they were using.

"All right ladies. Let's go," he said.

When he opened the two doors on the passenger side, Maria jumped into the front seat. He was a little disappointed that Bailey had to sit in the back, but at least he could see her in the mirror.

The ride to his home was short. How was he going to get Bailey alone? He wanted to greet her properly with a kiss and a hug.

Once inside, he opened the cabinets under his countertop bar. There, he kept serving pieces and mixing bowls.

"What have you got that we can use?" Bailey said. She squatted down beside Maria. "Do we need a chaffer?"

"No because we will all eat together," Maria said.

Maria pulled out some frying pans, a couple of larger pots and lids. Bailey pulled out a set of mixing bowls, and measuring cups and spoons.

"What about this?" Maria pulled out some cookie sheets.

"Yes. And we need spatulas and spoons," Bailey said.

Michael went to another room to retrieve large plastic containers to put all this equipment in. When he returned, the ladies seemed to be finished.

"Here you go, ladies," he said.

"Perfect," Bailey said. She started loading the containers with the equipment.

"Do you have a restroom I can use?" Maria asked.

"Certainly." Michael pointed across the kitchen to a door.

"Thanks." Maria headed to the room and stepped inside.

Michael grabbed Bailey's hand and pulled her to him. He kissed her tenderly and she returned the kiss. He didn't want to stop but Bailey put a hand on his chest. He whispered in her ear. "I wanted to give you a proper greeting," he said.

She touched his cheek and stiffened when the sound of a door opening stopped her. She dropped her hand to her side.

"Almost done," she said.

"I'll take this one out to the car," Michael said.

Maria helped Bailey with the last container when Michael left.

"So, what's going on between you two?" Maria asked.

5

SUSPICIONS

Bailey's heart pounded. "What do you mean?"

"I see the way he looks at you," Maria said.

"Do you have the second container full yet?" Michael asked, coming into the room.

"Yes. It's full," Maria said.

"Are you two ready, then?" he asked.

"Yes," Maria said.

"I'm ready," Bailey said. Now what should she do? Admit to having an affair with the owner of the hotel? Or should she just ignore the comments? Ignoring the comments would be hard since she had to work with Maria for the next several weeks.

Once they got to the car, Maria let herself in on the front passenger side. Bailey was beside the car's back door.

"Maria suspects something between us," she whispered into his ear and pulled the back door open.

Michael closed the trunk and opened the driver's side.

Bailey had climbed inside and buckled up before Michael got into the car.

Once he pulled onto the main road, he started a conversation with Maria.

"So, Maria, are you the head housekeeper at your property?"

"Yes, I am."

"How long have you been doing that?"

"For several years, now," she said.

"And do you like it?"

"Yes, most of the time."

Bailey sat back and listened to their conversation. What if Maria asked her more questions? What would she say?

Before she realized it, they were back at the hotel. Maria got out her door before Michael could open it. Bailey took her time getting out and he held her door for her.

"Hey, why did you hold her door and not mine?" Maria asked.

"Well, it's hard to be a gentleman when a woman doesn't know how to be a lady," he said.

Maria's brows furrowed at that and she headed inside the lobby.

"Can I help you, Michael?" Bailey asked.

"These are too heavy for you, Bailey, but you can get the door for me."

"I'd love to." She hurried through the automatic entrance doors and opened the door to the kitchen. She waited for Michael.

"Where's Maria?" he asked.

"I don't know. I think your comment affected her somehow."

He pulled Bailey toward him and leaned against the door. He wrapped his arms around her and she hugged him back.

This is where she wanted to be, in his arms. She was growing accustomed to his presence and felt more relaxed each time she was around him. She leaned against his chest and inhaled his scent.

Someone pushed against the door, banging into Michael's heels. He released Bailey and opened the door.

"Sorry. I didn't know you were in here," Maria said.

"I brought in one of the boxes. Where else would I be?"

"Uh, I don't know."

"Well, I'm off to get the second box. I'll be right back."

"Do you think we should unpack the two containers and put stuff away?" Bailey asked. She opened the container.

"No, let Linda do that. She needs to know where everything is," Maria said.

"She'll have all those groceries to put away. I think I'll stick around and help her," Bailey said.

"Suit yourself. I'm going up to my room." Maria pulled the door open and Michael stood on the other side.

"Just in time," he said.

"See you in the morning, Maria," Bailey said.

Maria headed to the elevator area.

After Michael set the container down, he took Bailey's hand and caressed it. "What did she say to you?"

"She's suspicious that something is going on between us. I don't know what to say to that."

"Always tell the truth," Michael said. He pulled her into another hug. "I have a feeling that tonight we'll be dreaming of each other instead of being together."

"Well, if it must be in dream form, let's do the bubble bath again," she said.

He lifted up her chin and kissed her more passionately, until someone pushed the door into his heels again.

"Oops. Didn't know anyone was in here," Larry said.

"We just brought in the pots and pans," Bailey said. She pulled the door open all the way.

Larry came in with several bags of groceries, followed by Linda.

"Here, Linda. Let me bring in the groceries while you put them away," she said.

"Great idea," Linda said. She set her bags down on the counter.

Michael walked out with Bailey and helped bring in bags of groceries as well. Once everything was out of the car, Michael gave Bailey a sweet kiss. "Until we dream tonight," he said.

"Until we dream," she whispered back. She watched him drive off and carried the last bag into the kitchen.

"Where's Larry?" Bailey asked.

"Oh, he must have gone to his room or something. I haven't seen him since we first came in," Linda said.

"Well, it looks like you've got everything squared away," Bailey said.

"Yes, even the pots and pans."

"Well, we just have to remember what goes back to Michael's house when our stuff comes in," Bailey said.

"I can make a list tomorrow," Linda said. "I'm totally wiped out tonight."

Linda and Bailey headed for the elevators. Once inside, Linda asked her a question she didn't want to answer.

"What time did you get back from cleaning up at Michael's yesterday?" she asked.

"I have no idea. I really didn't check. Why?"

"Well, Maria and I knocked on your door several different times and you never answered."

"Well, I slept really good yesterday."

When they reached Linda's room, Bailey said, "Good night."

She technically didn't lie and she did sleep well the night before. In fact, it was the best sleep she had in years.

Bailey sat at her computer and worked on fleshing out her story. She worked from her premise and created her log line. From there, she continued writing for a couple hours when she decided to call it quits. She quickly showered and got ready for bed. When she curled up under the covers, she heard Michael's voice.

"Hello love. I'm thinking of our bath time together."

"Me, too, Michael. I can't wait 'til we do it again."

Then she thought about her time with Michael and re-lived the sensations all over again.

The next morning, Bailey dressed quickly and went downstairs to see if Linda needed help with breakfast. She had set her alarm for 6 a.m., which was the time breakfast was served at the Hudson, but they'd all been up around 8 a.m. since they got here.

Just before entering the kitchen, Bailey noticed some men moving big cabinets in an alcove area beside the kitchen. She realized that's where the food would be served. "You gentlemen are early today," she said.

"We've got a lot of cabinets to unload today," one of them said.

"Well, that's good news for us." She opened the door and found the kitchen dark. "Hmm." Linda must be running late.

Bailey made some coffee in a small coffee pot that Michael lent them. She didn't know what Linda had planned to cook, so she left the kitchen and headed to the meeting room. It would be a few minutes before the coffee was finished anyway.

She turned on some lights in that room as well, but no one was there. Glancing at her watch, she realized it was only 6:30 a.m. Larry did want them there early but he didn't say how early. While in the meeting room, she opened the hall door and the side door so she could see when someone came down the hall from the elevators. Then she headed back into the kitchen to see if the coffee was ready.

Bailey found some paper cups for the coffee and found Linda's menu in the cabinet. She pulled it out and rolled up her sleeves. She could handle this. After all, she had been cooking since she was ten years old.

While she was cooking the scrambled eggs, she had some bacon in the convection oven on the cookie sheets. She pulled out a loaf of bread and set it up next to the toaster. She debated on toasting it, or letting everyone toast their own bread, but that would be too many people in the kitchen. She decided to try it in the oven on another cookie sheet.

Now, she thought those chaffers would come in handy, but they didn't bring one. Once everything was done, she covered everything in foil and let it sit in the oven to stay warm.

She glanced at her watch. It was after 7 a.m. She headed into the lobby to see if she could find anyone, carrying some paper plates, plastic forks, and napkins. She saw the men still working on the cabinets, but no one in the meeting room. Once she set everything down, she texted Larry to let him know breakfast was ready. But she didn't have the numbers of her team mates.

Within a few minutes, Larry came down to the meeting room and was followed by Ted and Maria.

"Where's Linda?" Bailey asked.

Larry glanced around. "Didn't she fix breakfast?"

"No, I did. You never told us how early you wanted us here," Bailey said.

Larry glanced at his phone. "She didn't respond to my text. Maria, go check on Linda," he said.

Maria left the room.

"Did you want me to bring the food out here, or let you go into the kitchen and help yourself?" Bailey asked.

"Just bring it out here," Larry said.

Bailey headed back to the kitchen and found the bowls she brought from Michael's and put the food into the bowls. Before she could leave the kitchen, the door opened.

"Good morning love," Michael said.

She smiled. "Good morning! What are you doing here so early?"

"I've got the cabinets coming in today. I see they are here already. I need to make sure they put them in the right places in the rooms."

"Grab a bowl and help me take these to the meeting room, please?"

Michael moved in front of her, lifted up her chin and gave her a kiss. With her hands full, she couldn't hug him.

"Now it's a good morning," Michael said.

She smiled and headed to the meeting room. Michael followed her with the toast.

"Did you fix breakfast?" he asked.

"Yes. I didn't know where Linda was, so I got it started."

Maria passed them in the lobby. "You don't have coffee?" she said.

"Oh, yes, it's in the kitchen," Bailey said.

"I'll get it," Maria said.

Once everyone was in the meeting room, they sat together and ate breakfast.

"Isn't Linda coming?" Bailey asked.

"She was sick this morning. She threw up and her stomach is messed up," Maria said.

"Does she want me to fix her a dish?" Bailey asked.

"She said she can't eat anything right now," Maria said.

"I think we'll start our mornings at 8 a.m.," Larry said. "This is a little earlier than I meant."

"Sure, breakfast at 8 a.m.," Bailey said. "I didn't know if we were going on Hudson hotel time."

"Today, Dave will be here to help get everyone logged on and set up. Next week, we'll be ready for any new hires to train," Larry said.

"Very good. I have the new General Manager coming in today and I'll let him get started on the ordering and inter-views," Michael said. He glanced at his phone. "It looks like the toilets and tubs just arrived and I've got the cabinet people here now." He patted Bailey on the back. "Lovely breakfast. Thank you for cooking."

"My pleasure," she said.

"I'll show the cabinet people where the cabinets go in the rooms while you're dealing with the tubs," Larry said. "When Dave gets here, the rest of you need to be here as well."

Bailey stood and started collecting paper plates and uten-sils. "I'll be working in the kitchen until he comes. Could one of you let me know when he arrives?" She glanced at Maria.

"Sure."

Michael grabbed a couple bowls and left with Bailey.

"I can't believe the two of them just sat there and didn't offer to pick up after themselves," Michael said.

"It gets frustrating sometimes. I was thinking that maybe

they're acting that way because they are out of their element. All three of them work hard at our hotel, but they are ready to leave right when the shift is up."

Bailey put the plates into the new trash can. It was small, but they would get a bigger one when the new GM started ordering supplies.

Michael set the bowls on the counter and gave her a kiss on the cheek. "Until later, love."

"I can't wait," she said. She stacked all the dirty dishes into the dishwasher and went back to retrieve the rest of the breakfast stuff and wipe off the table.

A couple hours later, Bailey was in the meeting room, notebook in hand, along with Ted, Maria, Linda, and Dave. They had all logged into their own computers. Bailey went over some refresher materials for the front desk, when Michael stuck his head in the door.

"I want you all to meet our new General Manager, Patrick Flynn."

Mr. Flynn shook hands with each of them and asked them to call him Patrick. Michael gave him a tour of the hotel and then showed him the office.

By lunchtime, everyone was ready for a break. Ted made the sandwiches without complaining. Linda went to show him where everything was and helped clean up.

"Do you think Larry will let us off this weekend?" Maria asked.

"I don't know. He said today was the start of our work week," Bailey said.

"Well, I want to get out of this hotel while I'm here and go somewhere," Maria said.

"I'd like to see more of Ireland as well." Bailey said.

. . .

Later in the day, while Maria prepared dinner, Larry spoke to the rest of them in the meeting room.

"I'll be working with the cabinet people again tomorrow and Saturday. Michael will be working with the new GM in his office in between working with the plumbers. We're giving you Sunday off. I plan on going to Galway if any of you want to join me."

Bailey's hopes went up at what Larry said. She wanted to spend more time with Michael, but was Michael available? She hadn't seen him much since lunch, but knowing he was here made her happy.

"We can finish up the computer work tomorrow," Dave said.

"I figured as much, but you'll be meeting with the new GM on Saturday, going over job descriptions and lists of what your departments might need," Larry said.

Michael came into the room. "Well, the plumbers have left for the day."

"And the cabinet people," Larry said. "I told the group they could have Sunday off. I plan on going to Galway for the day and anyone who wants to, can join me."

"Brilliant. We start again on Monday, then?" Michael asked.

"At 8 a.m. sharp."

Bailey exchanged phone numbers with Linda, Ted, and Dave. She would get Maria's number when dinner was ready.

"I'm going to check on Maria and see if she needs help in the kitchen," she said. Since they were winding down on the day, she wanted to make herself useful. When she got to the kitchen, Maria was finishing up with the meal.

"Do you need help?"

"Oh, yes! I can use some help getting the food out to the meeting room."

Bailey gathered the plates and plasticware and headed back to the meeting room to get it ready for the food.

Michael came up to her and helped her move some papers to make room for the meal.

"We can use more hands to bring the food out," she said.

Michael raised his hands. "Will these do?"

"Oh, yes." She walked out with him into the empty lobby.

"How was your day, Bailey?" he asked.

"More productive than the past few days."

Michael opened the kitchen door for her.

"Thank you, Michael," she said. She stepped into the room.

Maria handed her some bowls of food. "Thank you for what?"

"Michael held the door for me. I thought that was nice. I'm not used to that kind of treatment from men," Bailey said.

Maria handed Michael a couple of bowls and grabbed a pitcher of tea and a stack of cups. "I think that's it," she said.

The three of them headed back to the meeting room.

"Oh, Larry is giving us Sunday off and he's invited anyone who wants to go with him, to Galway," Bailey said.

"Oh, I do! I want to go!" Maria said.

"Be sure and tell him," Bailey said.

Bailey, Maria and Michael set things down on the table and everyone helped themselves.

After dinner, Bailey exchanged phone numbers with Maria. Michael stayed for a while, sitting next to Bailey. He leaned close and whispered, "Do you want to go on an adventure with me on Sunday?"

"Absolutely I do," she whispered back.

Maria got up to clean the table. Linda stood up and helped

her. Bailey was about to do the same, but Michael held her arm.

He leaned in again. "Let them do it this time," he said.

Bailey glanced at Michael and realized she had been cleaning up after all of them since she got there.

"Well, I'm calling it a night," Larry said.

"Good night Larry," Bailey called out.

"Yeah, me, too," Ted said.

"I guess I have no choice since you have the only key," Dave said. The two stood up and left.

Michael took Bailey's hand. "Let's go for a walk." He led her outside and they walked around the property.

"It's really looking good out here," Bailey said.

"'Tis that. And you as well." He pulled her into a hug and kissed her. She kissed him back and her body tingled from his touch. She wanted more of him.

"I'm taking you with me tonight," he said.

"I'm all yours."

6

SECRETS EXPOSED

Bailey and Michael walked to his car, which he parked along the side of the building.

"That's an unusual place to park," Bailey said.

"That's so we can get away from prying eyes."

"Ah, yes. Thank you," she said. She got into his car after Michael opened the door for her. By the time they got to Michael's house, Patrick rode up on his bicycle.

Michael opened her door for her. "Bailey will be staying the night, Patrick," he said.

"Hello, Patrick," Bailey said.

"Hello, Bailey. Nice to see you again."

"I've got an idea for fund raising," she began.

"Oh?"

"Well, in the States, people love their pets. I thought I would print out a flyer about pet portraits for a donation for the clinic. That way, people learn about it and become invested in its success."

"That's an interesting idea. Is there anything I can do to help?" Patrick asked.

"Well, I'll need some details about the clinic and then maybe you can help me distribute the flyers?"

"I'd love to," he said.

Michael unlocked the door and they all went inside.

"Let's have a drink," Michael said. "I feel we're getting close with the hotel and the banquet."

Patrick pulled out a bottle of Jameson whiskey, while Michael got three glasses down from the cabinet.

"Make mine small," Bailey said.

"Are you not a whiskey drinker?" Patrick asked.

"I'm a rum drinker."

Michael put his arm around her and pulled her close. "If you're going to remain in Ireland for any length of time, you need to learn to drink whiskey."

"Well, I do like Bailey's Irish Cream."

Patrick pulled out a bottle of her drink of choice.

"It does have whiskey in it, so that counts, Dad."

Michael looked at the bottle. "Brilliant!"

Patrick poured the three drinks and they toasted with "*Sláinte!*"

"Are you working tomorrow, Patrick?" Michael asked. They moved into the living room with their second drinks.

"Yes. I go in half past nine."

"That's early."

"Yes, but I get off early, too."

"Well, I met with Fionnuala and Mr. Daly the other day about the banquet fundraiser," Michael said.

"Not Fionnuala Findley," Patrick said.

Bailey glanced between the two men.

"I'm afraid so, Patrick. She's got the connections I need

for this fundraiser, but I called Mr. Daly to make sure I wasn't there alone."

"Just be careful, Dad. I don't trust that woman."

Bailey took a sip of her drink.

"Did you know Bailey is an author?" Patrick asked his father. He downed the last of his drink.

Michael gazed into her eyes. "That's a new talent I didn't know about."

Patrick stood up. "Well, I'm heading to bed. Good night, Bailey. Good night, Dad."

"Good night, Patrick," they said in unison.

Patrick glanced at the two of them, then shook his head. He headed up the stairs.

Bailey stood and picked up the empty glasses and headed into the kitchen with them.

Michael was right behind her. "Why do you do that?"

"Do what?"

"You are constantly cleaning up other people's messes."

She set the three glasses in the sink. "I think I've always done that. Someone's got to do it, right?"

He pulled her into his arms. "I love everything about you, Bailey." Then he kissed her sweetly on the lips.

"You, sir, are a good kisser. I could kiss you all night."

Michael took her hand and led her to his bedroom. "We are going to do just that," he said.

The next morning, Michael's chest against her back was warm. She didn't want to move.

His alarm went off. "Good morning, love," he whispered in her ear. Then he started kissing her neck.

"Oh, you keep doing that and we'll never get our day started," she said.

"I would love a day like that with you," he said.

"Be careful what you wish for," she said. "We've got to get showers and dress." She threw her blanket off and realized she had nothing on.

"We can save time by showering together," Michael said.

Once they were in the shower, it turned steamy in more ways than one.

"I think showering is no faster than taking a bath with you," Bailey teased. She dried herself off.

"I have to admit it's easier to make love to you in the tub," Michael said. He rubbed his hair with his towel.

They both dressed and headed to the hotel. Bailey glanced at her watch. It was after 7 a.m. "Hopefully Linda feels better today." She realized she hadn't put her phone on to charge during the night and pulled it out of her jacket pocket.

"Oh my gosh!"

"What's the matter?" Michael asked.

"My phone is about dead but Linda texted me around 6 a.m. saying she was throwing up and couldn't make breakfast."

"We'll be there in a couple minutes. I'll help you."

She reached over and touched his cheek. "That's so sweet of you. Thank you."

He pulled into the parking area in front and opened Bailey's door again. Just as they entered the lobby, Maria was approaching the kitchen.

"I knew it!" Maria said.

"You knew what?" Bailey asked.

"You two are having an affair!"

Michael opened the kitchen door. "What makes you think that?"

"You just pulled up together in your car. Don't tell me you aren't," she said.

"Are you cooking breakfast this morning?" Bailey tried to change the subject.

"Linda couldn't reach you so she texted me."

"I forgot to put my phone on the charger last night." This was true since she didn't have the charger with her.

"I could use your help," Maria said.

"And I can use your discretion—" Bailey felt a hand on her shoulder. Michael stood beside her and gave her a squeeze-like hug.

"Maria, Bailey and I are seeing each other, yes, but it has nothing to do with your jobs or duties here. I will speak to Larry, who is your boss. You are all here to help my team get a good start. Once my new GM has everything under control, I will step back and let him run the hotel and Larry will oversee the financial part of things and I will remain his partner. Now if you need help, Bailey and I are here to help you."

"Uh, sure," Maria said. She reached for the menu and the three of them got breakfast cooking.

Nothing was said again about her and Michael, but after they ate, Bailey helped Maria in the kitchen with cleanup.

Bailey took out the meat she would use for dinner so it could thaw and set it in the sink.

Michael and Larry went about their business, and Dave and Ted went over some strategies for fixing computer problems.

Patrick Flynn arrived about 9 a.m. and headed to his office through the lobby. Bailey and Maria were heading back to the meeting room, carrying a pot of coffee.

"Hello, Patrick. Would you like some coffee?" Bailey asked.

"I'd love some," he said.

"We have some cups in the meeting room." Bailey said.

The three of them entered the room and Bailey poured him some coffee.

"I have some interviews this afternoon," Patrick said. "I'd like to go over some details on job descriptions with each of you, one at a time, if you don't mind?" Patrick said.

"We're ready when you are," Maria said.

"Great! Let's start with Ted," he said. He and Ted left the room and went to Patrick's office.

"You know, I think the front desk will probably be in front of his office when the workers get to that point," Bailey said.

"I wonder where the laundry facilities will be, and if I'll have an office," Maria said.

Dave stood and approached the two of them as they looked out into the lobby from the side entrance. "I have some things I need you two to finish on the computers," Dave said.

"Sure," Bailey said. She and Maria went back inside the meeting room to work on their programs.

Ted entered the room. "Maria, it's your turn."

Maria stood up and headed to the office.

"Since you've finished up all your work, Ted, I'm not sure what to do with you," Dave said.

"I'll see if I can find Larry or Michael. Maybe I can help with the cabinets or something." Ted left the room.

"Well, I think I'm finished with my stuff, too," Bailey said. "I think I'll check on Linda and see how she's feeling."

"Once Linda and Maria finish their refresher programs, we'll be ready for the new hires," Dave said.

Bailey took the stairs and knocked on Linda's door.

When she opened the door, Linda looked disheveled.

"Are you all right?" Bailey asked.

"No. I don't know why I'm sick. I feel awful."

"Is it something you ate?"

"Did anyone else get sick?" Linda asked.

"Everyone else seems fine."

Linda opened the door and let Bailey into her room.

"Are you still throwing up?"

"Yes."

"I can bring you some water or something to drink," Bailey said.

"I'm drinking water, but it makes me want to throw up again."

"When did you start feeling better yesterday?" Bailey asked.

"It was around lunchtime," Linda said.

Bailey felt her forehead. "You don't have a fever."

"Why am I just getting sick in the morning?" Linda asked.

Then it hit her. "Oh, my gosh!"

"What?"

"You're pregnant," Bailey said.

"What? No… I," Linda hesitated. Then she went through her purse and pulled out a calendar. She thumbed through it and counted some days. "Oh, no!"

"Well, that's good news, don't you think?" Bailey said.

"Yes, but very unexpected. I should see a doctor to make sure," Linda said.

"Yes, you should. But maybe we can find you a test first before you get your hopes up."

"That would be great. I don't want to tell my husband anything until I'm sure."

"I'll see if I can get to town and check the store for a test," Bailey said.

"The store is a lot farther away than Michael's house."

"Hmm, maybe I can get a ride from Michael, then."

"Don't tell anyone until I know for sure," Linda said.

"Oh, the GM wants to talk to each of us about our job descriptions. Are you feeling up to it?"

"Not really, but I'll get dressed. Maybe this nausea will go away by then."

"Okay, I'll come and get you when it's your turn," Bailey said. She headed to her room next door and put her phone on the charger. If she had time tonight, she needed to work on her story.

By the time she got downstairs, Maria had come back from speaking to Patrick.

"How did it go?" Bailey asked.

"Fine. He showed me where the laundry room was and the office I will use to work with the new housekeepers. It's nice and roomy. He wants to talk to Linda next."

"Well, I'll go next because Linda was just getting ready. She's still not 100 percent yet."

"Wow. I hope I don't get what she has," Maria said.

"No. I hope you don't either." Bailey took the job description papers she had next to her computer and went to speak to Patrick.

"Hello Patrick," she said. "I didn't know this was back here." She glanced around the office. There wasn't much room except for one comfortable chair for guests, a nice desk with a printer and desktop computer and the desk chair. Beside the desk was a cabinet. Part of it had bookshelves and part had doors for storing things.

"Cozy, isn't it?"

"Yes, it is," she said.

"Where's Linda?"

"She wasn't feeling well this morning but she'll be coming down shortly. I thought I would go next to save you time," Bailey said.

"That's fine. Let me show you the laundry and break room."

"Oh? I didn't know we had a break room," Bailey said.

Patrick escorted her through a small alcove. "This will be the offices for Housekeeping and Breakfast." He pointed to her left. There was nothing there yet. Then he turned and opened a door to another room. "Here is our laundry facilities." It was broken up into sections, with a large wall dividing each section.

"One side will be for mops and cleaning supplies for housekeeping or whoever needs them. The other side will have four washers, two to a wall. On the other side, we'll have four dryers. In the middle of each section will be tables for folding sheets and towels."

"What's at the end?" she asked.

"That's our break room, where people can have their lunch or dinner, depending on the shift."

"That's nice."

"Yes, once the training is over, we'll use this break room."

"You mean, once they finish it, right?"

"Absolutely."

She followed Patrick back to his office, then handed him her job descriptions. "I brought all three shifts with me. Each shift has similar jobs, but then each shift may have a job the others don't do," she said.

"And you've worked all three shifts?"

"Yes. Now as far as audit goes, what is printed out

depends on what reports you want to deal with and keep as well as what your accountant might need."

"I see. I'll look over these job descriptions and use that with my interviews. Do you need copies?"

"I have another set for each shift."

"Great. Did you want to send Linda in? I hope she's feeling better."

"I hope so, too. She was getting ready before I came."

Bailey left the office and headed back to the meeting room. Linda was there, so she sent her to the GM's office.

"Where's Ted?" she asked Dave. Bailey glanced at her watch. It was almost lunchtime.

"He said he would find either Michael or Larry to see if he could help out," Dave said.

Maria stopped her work to listen in.

"I'll see if I can find him. He will be making our sandwiches today," Bailey said.

"Who's turn is it to cook tonight?" Maria asked.

"I think it's mine," Bailey said. "I guess I'd better get my stuff out so I can fix it." She headed into the kitchen to get her things ready for dinner. There, she found Ted, making the sandwiches.

"There you are! I was about to hunt you down when I remembered I'm cooking tonight."

"Yeah? What are you fixing?"

"I'm making chili. Hope you like it."

"Well, I do like chili," Ted said.

After she had all her stuff laid out, she pulled out a tray and helped Ted set the sandwiches on it. He grabbed a bag of chips.

"What about drinks?" Bailey asked.

"We've got water in the meeting room. Larry set a couple cases in there. We can drink that," Ted said.

"Okay. Tonight, I think I'll make some tea," Bailey said. The two of them headed into the meeting room with the food.

"Just in time," Larry said. He walked into the room, followed by Michael.

"Couldn't wait to have the best peanut butter and jelly sandwiches in Ireland," Michael said.

"I bet," Ted said with a laugh.

After they ate, Ted cleaned up the mess. Bailey followed him into the kitchen.

"I can clean this up, Bailey," he said.

"Oh, I know you can, Ted. I'm going to start making my tea. I'll come back in a little while and start the chili."

She got a pot of water boiling on the stove while Ted finished up in the kitchen.

"Larry said we can take off this afternoon since we're finished," he said.

"Great. Well, I will be in here, I guess."

Ted hung up his towel and left the kitchen.

She pulled out the cutting board while she was waiting for the water. She might as well get her vegetables cut up to save time later.

By the time she got her tea bags steeping in the water, Michael walked into the kitchen.

"Oh, hello, Michael. How's it going with the plumbers?"

He walked up to her and kissed her neck after giving her a hug.

"Well, we've got most of the rooms on the third floor done with tubs."

"What about toilets and sinks?"

"That will come later. We have them in the rooms, but not installed yet."

"Are they working tomorrow, since it's Saturday?"

"Yes, but not a whole day. Hopefully, we'll finish the tubs on that floor."

"It's exciting seeing how the hotel is changing every day," she said. She set her knife down and washed her hands. "Now I can give you a proper kiss and hug," she said.

She wrapped her arms around his neck and kissed his lips. He squeezed her tight and returned her kiss.

"What are you making?" he asked.

"Chili."

"Hmm, sounds good. Anything I can help you with?"

"I was going to brown the meat in one pan and the vegetables in another."

"Why not do both in one pan?"

"Well, the meat has to be drained. So, do you want to do the meat or the vegetables?"

"I guess I can do the meat," he said.

Together, they stood at the stove, each stirring a different pot.

"Did your husband ever cook dinner with you?" he asked.

"No, well, maybe once. I liked it, but he never offered again. I think it's more enjoyable if you have someone to talk to."

"Megan wouldn't let me in the kitchen. But when she had cancer, I cooked all her meals. She just gave up on cooking altogether."

"You know what would be good right now?" Bailey asked.

"What?"

"A glass of wine. I've always wanted to do that. I've seen it in commercials and some movies, where two people are cooking and enjoy a glass of wine together."

"It sounds romantic." He pulled her into a hug and kissed her cheek.

"Maybe we could do that at your house one night?" Bailey said.

"I would love that, but this Sunday, I had planned to take you for a ride in the country. We'll drive half a day and turn around and come back, so you can see some of Ireland."

"Oh, that sounds wonderful. Maybe we can have a picnic," Bailey said.

"Or, we could have an adventure!"

7

GROUP DYNAMICS

"**A**fter I clean up the kitchen tonight, could you take me to the store, Michael?"

"Sure, sure."

She didn't want to mention Linda's situation until they were away from the property. She enjoyed dinner with the group and quickly cleaned up the kitchen. Michael came in to help her after the rest of the group broke up and went to their rooms.

"What are we looking for?" he asked. He pulled into a parking spot at the store. He had turned off the car.

"A pregnancy test kit."

His mouth dropped open. "Are you pregnant?"

"No. I'm past that stage. It's for someone on the team."

Michael walked around the car to open her door.

"Are you sure?" he asked.

"Yes. It's been a couple years since I've had a period. But what if it was me? How would you feel?"

"Well, at first I was surprised, but I would be happy for you to have my baby." He pulled her into a hug and kissed her.

"Well, don't say anything to anyone yet. Linda wants to be sure before telling her husband."

He held her hand as they walked into the store. His hand was warm and strong and she felt the same tingling when she first met him and he shook her hand. She enjoyed his attention.

She searched the aisles until she found what she came for. When she went to pay for it, the pharmacist stared at the two of them.

"We're trying to get pregnant," Michael said.

The pharmacist's eyes widened.

She tried to keep a straight face while paying for the kit.

Once they were past the counter, she burst out laughing. She liked his sense of humor. He held her hand and gave it a squeeze. He drove her back to the hotel and waited for her to come back to the meeting room. No one was inside, so he sat at a table and waited.

Michael thought about his conversation with Larry earlier today. There wasn't much Larry could say or do actually, but he wanted him to know instead of finding out from someone else. He promised to be as discreet as he could but he planned on continuing his relationship with Bailey. Then he thought about the pregnancy kit for Linda. What if Bailey did get pregnant? It would change both of their lives since they both had grown children. How would their kids take the news? How would he adjust to a child at his age? It probably wouldn't be that bad for him, but for Bailey, she would have the most to deal with.

He needed to make this relationship permanent. Would she want to be married again? Would he have complications from his government? He needed to check into that before he proposed. He couldn't imagine his life without her. He looked forward to her company and he'd only known her a week.

Bailey walked into the room. "Did you miss me?"

"Yes, I did." He stood and gave her a hug.

"I love your hugs. I never grow tired of them," she said.

"Didn't your husband give you a hug every day?"

"No. I had to force him to hug me and it wasn't anything like your hugs. Yours seem to get more intimate the longer you hug me."

"I mean to do that," he said.

"Well, did you want to stay here with me tonight? You can check out the Hudson bed."

"I just might do that."

She pulled him by the hand and led him up the stairs to her room.

"Do you always take the stairs?" he asked.

"Usually, if I'm by myself. I like the exercise."

"Did Linda take the test yet?"

"She did. And she's pregnant."

"I hope that's good news for her," he said.

"Yes, but she said it was unexpected. They wanted children, but hadn't decided when to have them. They just got careless before her trip and had a 'fling,' she called it."

"I hope she isn't sick in the morning," he said.

"Well, if she is, I won't have to get up so early, but I can get the breakfast going."

"I'll help you, then."

She unlocked her door. "You would?" She pushed the door open.

"Sure, sure. I enjoy being in the kitchen with you."

She closed her door and locked it, then pinned him against the door. One hand was on his shoulder, the other caressed his cheek. He loved the way she touched him.

"You know, I think a man in the kitchen is very sexy." She said it so close to his lips he had to kiss her. He wrapped his arms around her and squeezed her into a tight hug. She hugged him back, running her arms up and down his back.

When he came up for air, she pulled him into the bedroom area and went straight to the window to close the curtains.

She walked back into his arms. "Now, where were we?"

He took her hand and walked into the bathroom. When he saw how small the tub was compared to his own tub, he shook his head. "This tub won't do."

"Not for what you want to do, but…" she pulled him into the bedroom area again and pulled down the bedding. "This will do nicely." She sat on the bed and patted a spot beside her.

"Well, if you insist," he said. He blinked his eyes, removing their clothes and jumped into the middle of the bed.

"I guess we'll have to make do." He pulled her into his arms and kissed, licked, and fondled her until she couldn't take it and then made slow, passionate love to her until he couldn't hold out any longer. She was easy to love and she loved him back the way he had always wanted to be loved.

Hours later, Bailey opened her eyes and glanced around the room. Where was she? And what time was it? Did she set her alarm? She felt the warmth of Michael's skin against hers. She turned in his arms to face him.

He kissed her. "Good morning love," he said.

"What time is it?" She snuggled next to him, not wanting to leave the warmth of his body.

"Time to get dressed."

She sat up and reached for her phone. It was 6:10 a.m. She didn't set her alarm and her phone was about to die. She plugged it into her charger and headed to the bathroom. "I'm going to take a quick shower," she said.

"I may join you shortly," he said.

After she washed her hair, the curtain opened and Michael stepped inside.

"It's cozy in here," he said.

"Yes. Not much room to move around. Turn around and I'll wash your back," she said.

He did as he was told and she soaped up the washcloth, washing his back and bottom.

"You keep that up and I won't let you leave," he said.

He turned around and she kissed him. "Your shower is roomier than this one. Let's wait until we get back to your place. I love the architecture of your house," she said.

"You know I designed it myself, right?"

"Yes, Patrick told me." She stepped out of the shower and grabbed a towel.

While she dried off, she continued the conversation. "So, how long have you been an architect?"

"About thirty years. I'm actually planning on retiring after building Patrick's clinic. I was just going to enjoy the earnings from the hotel and my retirement."

"That sounds lovely. You could travel, too."

"I had thought about that just a little, but traveling alone is not as much fun as traveling with someone." He pulled the curtain open and stepped out on the bathmat. She combed her hair and watched him dry off through the large mirror. His body was firm and muscular for a man his age.

"You must work out a lot to keep in shape," she said.

"I did until I met you, love."

"Oh? What did you do before you met me?"

"I have a gym in the back of my garage. Patrick and I use it on a regular basis. I can't go much longer without my workouts."

"I know what you mean. I usually work out at home and walk a lot but the lack of sidewalks makes it harder to do it here."

She left the bathroom to finish getting dressed.

"We'll have a gym here at the Hudson when we get all the rooms finished," he said. He came out into the room and blinked his clothes back on.

"Oh, that's right," she said. "After this weekend, we need to get back to our routines." She zipped up her jeans and slipped on a t-shirt.

"You look wonderful," he said.

"Thank you. You look scrumptious." She pulled him to her and kissed him. He returned the kiss and hugged her tight.

"I love mornings with you, Bailey. It makes my day."

"Hmm, I love hearing that." She grabbed her jacket and headed to the door. He beat her to it and unlocked it before holding the door for her.

"Thank you, sweetie," she said. She caressed his cheek.

"Sweetie?"

"Do you prefer honey?"

"I've never had a pet name before."

She walked toward the stairs and he reached that door before she got to it and opened it for her.

"Loverboy?"

"How about Michael?"

She wrapped her arm through his. "Okay, Michael, whatever you say."

She arrived in the kitchen with Michael and got started on the breakfast. With Michael's help, she was able to have everything ready before 8 a.m.

"Is everything ready to go out?" Michael asked.

"Yes. All we need to do is text Larry." She reached into her pocket and couldn't find her phone. "My phone!"

"You left it on the charger, love."

"I did. Can you text Larry and have him text everyone?"

"Sure, sure."

Bailey carried the large tray of food out to the meeting room and set it near the plastic ware and paper plates Michael had already set out. She headed back to get the rest of the food, but Michael met her half way. She took some of his burden and went back to the meeting room with him.

"So, I noticed you called me love but you didn't like my nicknames for you?"

"What's wrong with love?"

She wrapped her arms around him. "Nothing is wrong with love." She put her hands on both his cheeks and looked him in the eyes. "As long as I can call you love, too."

He kissed her again. "I'm good with that."

Maria walked into the room just as she pulled away from Michael.

"Is Linda still sick?" Maria asked.

"I guess so. When I came down, she wasn't in the kitchen, so I started breakfast. Michael helped me."

Maria raised an eyebrow and glanced at both of them. She knew better, but Bailey wasn't going to argue this morning.

Shortly after, Dave and Ted walked in, followed by Larry.

"So how are we doing on the computer work?" Larry asked.

"Everyone is caught up here. We're just waiting for the new hires," Dave said.

"I think if we want to finish the tubs on the third floor today, maybe I can get you and Ted to help with that while Bailey and Maria sweep up the bathrooms so they can put the toilets in next week," Larry said.

"I thought you were doing the cabinets?" Michael asked.

"I am. We have about six or eight to go," Larry said.

"Well, we have the plumbers coming in shortly to do the tubs. I suggest Dave and Ted help with the cabinets. And Bailey and Maria can sweep the rooms that are finished."

"That'll work," Larry said. "Let's eat. If we get finished early enough, we'll take the rest of the day off," Larry said.

Patrick Flynn came in before they finished up and joined them. "I've got a few more interviews today and hopefully, we'll have a full crew ready to start on Monday."

"Brilliant," Michael said.

Bailey recruited Maria to help her clean up in the kitchen so they could get to the sweeping early. She was excited to have time alone with Michael.

"I'm looking forward to tomorrow," Maria said.

"Are you going with Larry to Galway?"

"Yes. Aren't you going?"

"Well, Michael said he would take me for a ride in the country so I could see Ireland."

"Well, I hope you have fun," Maria said.

"Whose turn is it to cook tonight?" Bailey asked.

Maria pulled out the menu they made. "Looks like Michael or Larry."

"Oh, boy."

"Should we flip a coin?" Maria asked.

"We need to let them choose." She hung up her towel and grabbed a broom and a dustpan. Maria grabbed the second broom and dustpan.

"We'll need a trash bag to put the debris in," she said. She pulled one from the roll. It was the larger size bag. "This should do. Where do we start?"

"I say let's find the owners first and figure out supper. Then you can start on one side of the hall and I'll do the other," Maria said.

"Good idea."

Maria looked through the rooms on the right and Bailey looked through the rooms on the left. She hoped she would find Michael, just so she could see him.

"I found Larry," Maria said. She stuck her head out into the hall. Bailey headed her way.

Larry was on the phone with someone, but he glanced at both of them as they stood in the doorway. He put his phone up and came toward them.

"Hi Larry," Maria started. "It's either you or Michael who will be cooking supper tonight."

"We have a change in plans."

"Oh?" Bailey asked.

"Linda has decided to go home to the States. She has a flight out of Shannon tonight. I'll have to take her to the airport. I can take some of you with me if you want to grab something to eat on the way there or back."

"Count me in," Maria said.

Dave and Ted came out from the bathroom. "Hey, we're in," Ted said.

"Okay, let's get this floor done so we can leave," Larry said.

"Wait a minute," Bailey said. She felt someone come up behind her. "Who will be training the new breakfast people?"

"You and Maria will have to take turns doing that," Larry said.

"And what about fixing breakfast the remainder of our time here?" she asked.

"You're doing a great job, Bailey. Do you mind continuing?"

She dreaded that. She had the front desk training to deal with as well. "We'll have to make another menu and buy groceries for next week," she said.

"We should have enough food for a couple more days. We'll deal with it then." Larry turned away to help Ted and Dave finish the installation of the bathroom sink cabinet.

Bailey felt a hand on her shoulder and turned around.

"I'll help you, love." Michael stood behind her. "I heard your voice. What's happening?" he whispered.

"Linda is going home tonight, so Maria and I will have to do our training as well as Linda's," she said. She pulled him down the hall, away from the room Larry was in.

"And you got stuck with breakfast?"

She took a deep breath and let it out. "Yes, but I can handle it. I just don't know it as well as Linda, especially the ordering part."

"Patrick Flynn will help you with that. He's worked every job in the hotel. I'm sure he can help you figure things out. That's why I hired him."

She smiled and patted his cheek. "Thank you, love. I needed to hear that." She walked down the hall and started with the first room on the left. She swept the dirt and debris out of each bathroom, working her way down the hall. She finished all the rooms on her side and then came up to the last two. Michael was inside, supervising the plumbers while they set the tub and hooked up the pipes to the faucets and handles. Then they installed the shower head.

"Hello, love. We're ready for Larry to install the cabinet for the sink. Can you find him?"

"Sure." She turned and headed across the hall, looking for Larry.

"There you are. Michael is ready for the cabinet installation," she said.

"Good. We've just finished this room," Larry said. Ted and Dave followed behind him.

She looked for Maria but couldn't find her. Bailey headed to her own room to use the bathroom. When she finished, she checked on Linda.

"How are you feeling?" she asked.

"I'm still sick in the morning. I had my husband call my doctor to set up an appointment for when I get home. I need something for this morning sickness."

"Good luck with that. I'm glad I didn't have it that bad while I was pregnant," she said.

"I'm all packed. I'm just waiting for Larry."

Bailey gave her a hug. "Have a safe trip, in case I don't see you before you leave."

"Thank you."

Bailey headed back to finish her sweeping. She found Maria in the hall. "I searched for you. Where did you go?"

"I went to my room to use the bathroom."

"Ah, me, too. I've got two more rooms. How about you?"

"The same. Larry is across the hall working on that room." Maria pointed to the room she had seen Michael in.

Maria went inside the room Larry, Ted and Dave just vacated and swept it clean. "Now, I'm down to one room," she said.

"I stopped to see Linda. She looks like this morning sickness has worn her out."

"Did you have that when you were pregnant?" Maria asked.

"Not like that. I was nauseous, but I could function."

"Me, too," Maria said.

The plumbers came out of the last room with their tools. Michael walked them to the elevators.

Within minutes, Larry, Ted and Dave left the room they were in and Bailey headed inside to sweep. It took them longer to install the cabinet, then it took the plumbers to install the tub and hook everything up.

After an hour, all the rooms were done. Bailey took the two brooms and dustpans downstairs and put them up. She realized she hadn't seen Michael since the plumbers left.

She checked on Patrick, the GM, and he was finishing up an interview.

"I'm sorry, Patrick. I didn't mean to bother you. I didn't know if you needed coffee or anything."

"Thank you for thinking of me Bailey," he said. He glanced at his watch. "It's lunchtime. I'm actually done for today. I've got several new hires coming in on Monday for training."

"Oh, about that," she began. "Linda will be leaving for the States tonight."

"Oh? Anything wrong?"

"She's been sick. Turns out she's pregnant, so I'll be doing the 'hands on' training for breakfast as well as the front desk. I'll just have to plan it for different times."

"Well, the front desk people should be training on the

computers for a couple weeks, so you can do the breakfast training during that time."

"I'm not too familiar with the ordering, but I can show them how to get breakfast ready. Especially if they want to really cook, they can come in at 7 a.m. when I have to fix breakfast for everyone else."

"I think I'll start everyone off with the Hudsonality video, then the breakfast people will learn a little about the computer work and reports, especially how to read them and figure out the ordering. I can do that training with them since I started out working in the kitchen. I've even worked in Hudson restaurants, so I'm good there."

"Oh, thank goodness. Well, when you want me to give them 'hands on' experience, I'll be ready for that," she said.

"Well, I'll see you early on Monday, then. I'm having everyone here at 8 a.m.," Patrick said. He put some papers in his briefcase, closed it, and headed for the door.

Bailey left just before Patrick and headed back to her room. She wondered where everyone was. The hallway was very quiet. She decided to take a walk, looking through each doorway, since they still didn't have doors, just to make sure no one was in any of the rooms. By the time she got to the end of the hall where the team was staying, she heard doors banging.

"Are you coming with us, Bailey?" Larry asked.

"No, I think I'll work on my book," she said. She really wanted to see Michael. But she didn't know where he was.

One by one, everyone left their rooms, Dave and Ted, Linda, and Maria.

"Have fun everyone!" she said. "Safe travels, Linda," she waved.

Linda waved back and everyone headed to the elevators.

She unlocked her door and realized her phone was still on

the charger. She took it off and phoned her daughter to check in with her. After a ten-minute chat, she checked her texts.

Nothing there. Bailey opened her computer and began working on her story. She worked for a couple hours and realized she was hungry and hadn't eaten lunch. She saved her work and decided to head downstairs and make a sandwich, but before she left the room, her phone rang. It was Michael.

8

FUN AND GAMES

"**H**ello love. Pack your bags. We're going on an adventure," Michael said.

"I love the sound of that. What do I need? A dress, jeans?"

"Both. I'll pick you up in about ten minutes."

Bailey took her small, overnight bag she used for toiletries and put a couple changes of clothes, her pjs, and some toiletries inside, along with a pair of shoes. She could wear what she had on, but she grabbed her coat and camera bag. She had been here one week in the month of May and it was still cold and rained almost every day. Since she was inside most of the time, it didn't matter, but she realized she had no rain gear. Hopefully, Michael would have some.

She headed downstairs and waited by the entrance. When Michael pulled up, he opened her door and took her overnight bag. She clung to her camera bag as she stepped into his car, and he put her overnight bag in the trunk. Then he quickly locked up the hotel.

Before he took off, he leaned toward her and gave her a kiss. "Hello, love."

"I missed you," she said.

"I was busy making plans for us."

"What have you got planned?"

He left the property and headed left onto the road. "I wanted to show you the land I bought for Patrick's clinic. Once I finish the hotel, I'll start on his vetery."

The drive was a couple miles down the road. Michael pulled over and got out of the car. Bailey quickly took her camera out of the bag before he opened her door.

They walked to the side of the road and climbed a slight rise.

"I'll cut a road in here and build the vetery over there," he said. He pointed to a spot in the area.

"How big is this lot?" she asked.

"It's about five acres. If he wants, he can live here as well. He will also have room to board animals if he chooses to."

"This is nice," she said. She snapped a couple of pictures of Michael with the lot in the background. When she glanced around, she realized she could see the ocean from where she stood. "Oh, Michael! What a beautiful view!"

"Yes, tis. That's why I chose it. I'll have to give you the full tour of my home when we get back."

"Oh?"

"Yes, I have a similar view from my place, but you haven't seen it yet."

"I've seen your kitchen, living room, and bedroom, so far."

"Well, since you liked those, you'll love the rest of the house as well."

"I'm looking forward to it. Come here and let me get a picture of you with the ocean in the background," she said.

After she snapped the image, he pulled her close and pulled out his phone, taking a picture of the two of them.

"Send me that, please?"

"Sure, sure. Now we go onto our adventure," he said.

He took her hand and walked her back to the car. They were off again and drove along the coast for a couple hours. He pulled over on a bare grassy area, overlooking the ocean. After letting her out of the car, he pulled out an easel and a canvas, then a tool box. She helped him carry these a short distance from the car.

"I didn't know you liked to paint, Michael."

"Oh, yes. Megan didn't like it too much, but I would sneak out when she had things to do and I would paint different areas of Roundstone and the neighboring coastline."

Once he was set up, she started snapping pictures of the various flowers and plants with the ocean as a background. When Michael wasn't looking, she got some images of him, painting.

He worked for about an hour before stopping.

"Now, we're off to another adventure," he said.

"That was short. What did you paint?"

"I did a preliminary drawing," he said.

When she glanced at his work, she realized it was a sketch of her with her camera. "I love it."

He packed up his things and they got in the car.

"We only have a few hours of daylight left, so we'll head to the bed and breakfast. Tomorrow, I'll give you the full tour of Connemara."

"Oh, thank you, Michael. I look forward to it."

They drove on a short distance and parked at a B & B in another village. After checking in and settling into their room, she discovered they had their own bathroom.

"You need to see all of Roundstone as well, but I've

planned the Connemara tour because it's supposed to be sunny tomorrow," he said.

"Oh, that was thoughtful of you. I'll charge my camera tonight so I can get plenty of pictures."

"Let's go and check out this town," Michael said.

"I'm ready when you are." She took her camera and he led the way.

Walking down the street, she spied a gift shop across from Murphy's Pub. Maybe they would have some journals. "Let's check out that store." She pointed to it. "I need a notebook or journal to take notes."

"For your books?" he asked.

"Yes. I want to write my feelings and experiences of Ireland so I can capture it in my book." The door jingled when she stepped inside.

"Hello there," a dark-haired Irish woman said when she entered.

"Oh, hello," she said.

"Oh, hello Michael!"

Bailey turned toward Michael. "This is Mary, Megan's sister," he said.

"Oh, nice to meet you, Mary," she said.

"This is Bailey Jackson. Bailey is helping to train our new employees at the Hudson Inn in Roundstone," he said.

"Brilliant," Mary said. "I'll come visit when you have it opened."

The place had a few people inside, looking around.

"I'm looking for a small notebook or journal. Do you have any?" she asked Mary.

"Toward the back corner," she said.

She found the spot and browsed the shelves when she heard the door jingle again. *This is it. One of her dreams.*

"Hide me, quick!" Michael said in a panicky voice.

Bailey glanced up as Mary escorted him past her, toward the back. He paused long enough to hold a finger up to his lips, motioning her to be quiet.

Her breath caught in her throat. This dream happened before she met Michael. Something was off. Her heart fluttered and she released her breath. She heard a commotion at the door. By that time, Mary rushed past her.

"Where is he, Mary?" an Irish woman demanded.

"We know he's in here. We saw him come in," another voice said.

Bailey found a journal she could use, but stayed in the back of the store, listening. She knew what would happen next.

"Back there," someone said. "Come on."

Bailey stepped out from the back aisle, into the path of three large women.

"Excuse me," Bailey said, holding her ground.

One woman tried to go around her, but Bailey stepped into her path.

"Pardon," the woman said. She pushed Bailey aside.

"Excuse me!" Bailey raised her voice louder than she ever had before. She kept the woman from passing.

The woman stopped in her tracks.

"We're trying to pass, miss. Step aside," another woman said.

"This is the back of the store, there's no other place you can go," Bailey said.

"This is none of your business, miss. Step aside."

Bailey caught a glimpse of Mary. "Well, in the States, if someone tried to go into *my* stockroom, I'd have them arrested for trespassing," she said loud enough for Mary to hear.

"I'll ring for the Garda," Mary said.

The tallest woman turned to face Mary. "You wouldn't!"

"Aye, but I will," she picked up the phone and began pressing buttons.

"Come on, ladies," the tall woman said as she led the others to the door.

"This is the last time we shop here," the last one said.

Mary followed her to the door and flipped the sign to 'Closed' and fastened the lock. "As if you ever shopped here before," she mumbled.

Bailey stood at the register and waited for her.

"That was brilliant!" Michael said, coming up to the register.

Bailey turned at the sound of his voice.

Michael grabbed Bailey's arms and pulled her to his chest, hugging her. She clumsily reached around his back, hugging him.

He was warm and he smelled good. Her heart fluttered and a warm feeling shot through her to her core, stirring those feelings she got every night, just thinking about him.

"Brilliant," he whispered. "Just like our dream."

His breath stirred those tingles down her spine, making them more intense.

He slowly pulled away, but kept his hands on her arms.

"I owe you, love," he said. He winked and smiled at her.

She swallowed hard as Mary rang up her journal. What was Mary thinking about this exchange? She handed her card to Mary.

Michael took her hand and held it. She felt safe.

"Why were those women after you?" she asked. She kept her gaze on him while he still held her hand.

"Don't you know, Bailey? He's the most eligible bachelor in these parts," Mary said.

"Well, that's your problem," Bailey said.

He cocked his head. "What do you mean, love?"

"They know you are eligible. If they knew you weren't, maybe they would leave you alone."

He pulled her to his chest again, hugging her more intimately, stroking her back.

"Brilliant. Simply brilliant."

She had an arm around his waist, clutching her camera bag in the other hand. She wanted to stay like this, safe in his arms.

"I owe you, love. Let's go get some dinner." He gazed deep into her eyes.

"Well, I am hungry," she said. Her heart did flip flops in her chest. She loved his attention, especially in public. She never got that from her husband.

"Where will you be eating tonight?" Mary asked.

"Murphy's," Michael said.

"I wouldn't let this one out of your sight, then. If she can stand up to those three, you'll be safe," Mary said. She followed them to the door and unlocked it. "It never fails."

"What's that?" Bailey asked.

"When Michael comes to town, the word spreads fast. He never has a moment's peace."

Bailey glanced up at him. "I guess I'll have to fight them all off, then."

After Mary let them out of the store, they headed across the street for Murphy's. Not only did she re-live one of her dreams, but she was heading for a pub where another dream took place. Nervousness and excitement ran through her.

"You know, Michael, I haven't had one of our dreams since our first night together. And now, I just had one dream come true."

"We were meant to do these things, Bailey. I'm enjoying this, aren't you?"

"Yes, I am."

She hesitated at the door. She looked forward to her dream each night, but now it was playing out. Was she ready for this?

The thought of his embrace and his kisses made her want to play along, even if she knew what was in store for her. Was it wrong to want this man? Was it wrong to want to be desired once more as a woman? Could this be her second chance at love?

She took a deep breath. If this was only a temporary fling, she would at least leave Ireland after being kissed by an Irishman. *God help me.* Michael pulled the door open and she stepped inside.

Bailey glanced around the darkened pub. "This looks just like the pub in my dreams," she said.

"Aye, it does," Michael said. He guided her to a seat at the bar. The place was busy for late afternoon.

"Hello there, are you having a meal or a pint?" the bartender asked.

"Well, can we have both?" she asked.

"Sure, sure," he said. He handed each of them a menu.

She glanced over the menu and picked something out real quick. "I'll have this steak and a pint of Smithwick's."

"And I'll have the same except make mine a Guinness," Michael said.

"Good choice. I'll be right back."

She watched him punch in the order on the register and then he poured their drinks.

"Here you go." He slid the drinks toward them.

"Thanks," she said. She took a sip. Hmm. It reminded her of the Cherokee Ale she loved from the Brewery.

"You're not drinking a Guinness?" Michael asked.

She choked on her drink. "I don't like to wait that long to drink it. Have you tried a Smithwick's?" she asked.

"Not lately."

"Here, have a sip of mine." She moved her drink toward him.

He took a sip. "Not bad. But something as good as a Guinness is worth waiting for."

"Kind of like you," she said.

"What do you mean?"

"Finding a man like you was worth waiting for."

He took her hand and brought it to his lips, kissing it. "And you, as well, love." He winked at her.

The bartender brought their meals and they ate, making conversation in between bites.

"Tomorrow, I hope to take you to a place where there's dancing. Do you like dancing?"

"I love it, but I haven't been dancing in years."

"Well, we should both do well, then," he said.

After the meal, Bailey glanced around looking for a restroom. When she spied the sign, she slipped off her stool.

"Watch my camera bag, please, Michael? I'm going to the toilet."

"Sure, sure, love. I'll be next after you."

The bartender slipped Michael the bill and he paid it.

"Michael Shaunessy! You've blessed me twice with your presence, love," Fionnuala said, sitting down next to Michael.

"That seat's taken, Fionnuala." *What was she doing here?*

"Yes, by me."

"No, I'm with Bailey Jackson. She's in the toilet at the

moment."

Fionnuala moved the camera bag and realized it was slightly open. "Oh, what have we here?" She pulled out the camera and inspected it.

"Now, put that back. It belongs to Bailey and I'm looking after it." He reached for the bag and the camera, but Fionnuala pulled away with both.

Fionnuala moved her purse to the other arm and fidgeted with the camera bag, while returning the camera. She leaned over the bar counter and gazed into his eyes.

"What do you see in this Bailey Jackson? Who is she and why are you with her?"

"She's a beautiful soul who writes romances and she happens to be my soul mate. What are you doing there? Leave her bag alone."

She fumbled with the zipper. "I can't seem to close this useless bag."

"Give it here." He took it away from her and zipped up the camera bag and put it beside him. "What do you want, Fionnuala?"

He knew she was up to something.

"I thought maybe I could come to your place and go over the details about the fundraiser."

"I'm busy this week. Maybe the coming week."

"Perfect. I'll call you, love."

"I'm back," Bailey announced. "Now it's your turn."

"Oh, Bailey, this is Fionnuala Findley, the manager of O'Malley's, in Limerick," Michael said.

"Nice to meet you." Bailey extended her hand.

Fionnuala glanced at her hand, then ignored her. She reached over and kissed Michael's cheek. "Later, love."

As soon as Fionnuala left, he wiped his face with his handkerchief. *Why did she have to spoil the evening?*

Bailey finished off her pint and watched Michael head to the toilet. What was that red-haired beauty doing with her dream lover? She wouldn't give her another thought. This was her night and she was going to enjoy it.

When he returned, she got off her barstool. He put his arm out and took her arm in his. "Are you ready for a night of passion, love?"

"Only if it's with you," she said.

Bailey gathered up her package from the gift shop, along with her camera bag, and left with Michael.

The walk back to the B & B was pleasant, even though it was cooling down. Michael gave her hand a little squeeze.

She caught her bottom lip with her teeth. She swallowed the lump in her throat. Bailey's heart sped up as they neared the B & B. The two pints of Smithwick's made her feel less anxious.

"So what do you do at this Brewery?" he asked.

"I'm a hostess. I seat people, sell beer and souvenir glasses and t-shirts and take to-go orders by phone."

"And do you enjoy it there?"

"Well, most of the time I do. I enjoy the people I work with but sometimes it's tiring keeping up with two jobs."

They approached their B & B and headed for the stairs.

"As I recall," he began, "We shared a passionate kiss at the door."

A thousand nerves exploded in sensations at once as Michael softly kissed her. Then, he deepened the kiss. Each time he kissed her, she marveled at how perfect his kisses were. Her body awakened with a desire she had only felt with Michael.

Never had a man kissed her so thoroughly, so intimately.

Thinking about all those years she had been married to a man who didn't like kissing…what a waste.

Michael opened the door and guided Bailey into the room. Taking her by the hand, he walked her to the bed. "We'll do this the old fashioned way," he said.

"Oh, and what's that?"

He kissed her again while trying to remove her shirt. He stopped only long enough to get the shirt over her head.

"Now it's my turn." Bailey had to unbutton Michael's shirt. Kissing him while unbuttoning his shirt was difficult, so he helped her.

Then, when it came to her pants, Michael took his time unzipping them and pulling them slowly down her legs. On his way up, he kissed her knees, then her thighs, her belly, then her chest, before kissing her lips. Her senses tingled at the anticipation of each touch.

When it was her turn, she took her time unzipping his pants, while caressing his shaft before removing his pants. He inhaled deeply at her touch.

When she came back up, she kissed his inner thighs and his belly, but kissed and licked his chest.

When it was his turn, he kissed her neck down to her breasts, taking time with each one after removing her bra. Bailey breathed heavily at his touch. When he moved down to her belly, he took his time moving to her core. She pressed her hands against his shoulders, to keep her balance. Her breathing became labored as she fought to keep from moaning loudly. When he finally stopped, she returned the favor with his shaft, caressing, licking and sucking until he stopped her.

Michael took her to bed and after more kissing, licking, and suckling the two came together in a passionate climax.

9

THE STORM

After spending a leisurely morning, snuggling, kissing and making love, Bailey got up and dressed for the day. She had fallen in love with Michael and wondered what would happen at the end of the training sessions. Would she head back to the States, never to see him again? She swallowed hard at the thought. She was a big girl now. She would think of this as a fling and be strong. Other women did this all the time, didn't they? But she didn't know of any woman who confessed having a fling like this. Was she too old for a 'fling'?

While Michael showered, she packed her bag and gathered her camera and things. She loved the way he treated her and talked to her. She hoped he felt the same about her. The one thing he hadn't said was that he loved her. He did call her 'love,' though. Did that count? Her husband only said he loved her once, and he had to be coerced into saying it. But once every twenty-six years was not enough.

When Michael was finished in the shower, he came out

with wet hair, rubbing it with the towel. "I'm sorry, love, but I think we missed breakfast."

"That's okay. Maybe we can grab something along the way," she said.

"I don't recall many places along the way, but before leaving town, we can stop at the bakery and purchase something for the trip."

"That sounds grand," she said. She remembered he used that term a few times.

After finding the bakery, Michael bought some sweet rolls and coffee, along with a couple of sandwiches for later. They sat outside with their food and enjoyed the windy, but dry weather.

Michael took her to see Kylemore Abbey, Clifden Castle, and then did a walking tour of Clifden, looking for the perfect spot for a picnic. He stopped at a small pub and bought a couple of beers, while she used the toilet.

"Tonight, there will be an Irish group playing here at the pub," he said. "If you like, we can come back and listen to the music."

"Is it the kind of music we can dance to?" she asked.

"Not unless you know Celtic dancing," he said.

"Is that hard to learn?"

"It takes years to learn it, love."

"Well, I'd like to hear it if you like? We can go dancing another time, if you want?"

He kissed the side of her head. "I love that you are so adaptable, Bailey."

"You do?"

"One of your many charms."

"Thank you."

They found a nice spot, not far from the pub, and set a

blanket down before sitting together to enjoy their sandwiches.

The sun came out just for them and warmed her face.

"I'm enjoying this day, Michael," she said. She leaned back on her hands, her legs outstretched.

"Me, too, Bailey. I'd like to take another day to work on my painting, though."

"We only have tonight before I have to fix breakfast tomorrow," she said.

"I guess we'll plan another weekend adventure, then," he said.

"I'm looking forward to it." Her heart swelled with anticipation.

When they finished eating, they cleaned up their mess and packed the blanket back in the car. It was late afternoon.

"We can explore Clifden a little more and then we'll head back to the pub."

By the time they reached the pub, Bailey was looking forward to hearing Irish music. Michael bought them a couple pints of Guinness and they sat at a table where they could see the group of musicians. The music was wonderful and she had the feeling she belonged here. She snapped a few photos of the group and a few candids of Michael. Her ancestors came from Ireland and she felt at home. When the group took a break, her and Michael left and headed back to Roundstone.

"Thank you, Michael. I really enjoyed this adventure. I'd love to do this again." She carried her camera bag and suitcase into Michael's house.

He helped her with her bag after opening the door for both of them.

"I want to give you the full tour of the house," he said. He set the suitcases down in his bedroom and opened the curtains that ran across one wall.

Through the windows, she could see lights of the buildings across the road, but beyond them, the moon's glow shone on the ocean.

"Wow. I bet the sunsets are gorgeous," she said.

"They are, love. I want you to experience them while you are here." He closed the curtains on those set of windows and opened the curtains on the other side. The windows overlooked his garage and parking area and she noticed behind the garage was a set of mountains. "I didn't notice the mountains before. How nice. You get sunrises over here, don't you?"

"Yes. They are lovely, too." He led her through the dining room, and kitchen, then living room. Beyond that, he had an office with a desk and a drafting table with a large closet. "I sometimes paint on the back patio when the weather is nice," he said. He opened up the French doors to the patio.

"It's nice out here when it's not raining," she said.

"When Patrick moves out to his new home, I'll use his room for painting indoors." He led her toward the garage, and turned to face the house. "See, he has a great view from the second floor with a small balcony. I can paint with the windows open, on the balcony, or inside."

"That sounds wonderful, Michael. It's so good to have a place to call your own to do what pleases you."

"What about you, love?"

"What do you mean?"

"Do you have a place to do what you love?"

"I can write anywhere, but I do have an office where I write my books. I also love to do gardening, so that's always outside. I use one of my empty rooms for sewing and crafts. I guess I have many places to work in things I enjoy."

He led her back into the house where they ran into Patrick.

"Hello, Patrick," she said.

"Hello, Bailey, Dad. What are you two up to?"

"Giving Bailey the grand tour," he said.

"I just got back from O'Donnel's with some snacks. Would you like some?" Patrick asked.

"Oh, yes. I'm a little hungry," Bailey said.

"We'll make a meal of it," Michael said.

The three of them headed inside. Patrick set up the snacks on the bar, while Michael pulled some food out of the fridge and added to it. Patrick poured each of them a beer and they sat together at the bar and talked about the day.

"Tell me more about your fundraiser, Patrick," she said.

"The fundraiser will be a large, catered banquet at $1000 per plate. It will be held in Limerick later this month," he said.

"We're having the fundraiser for equipment before the building is finished so Patrick can start the day his vetery is complete," Michael said.

Patrick turned and stared at his father. "I thought it was for the building itself. Where will we put everything?"

"You order it ahead of time and have it delivered right before you open. You'll have the money to pay for it upfront. I've already got the financing for the building."

"Will you accept donations other than the banquet?" Bailey asked.

"Of course. Patrick has set up a website where donations can be made," Michael said.

"I'll work on the flyers tomorrow," Bailey said. She pulled out her phone and put in Patrick's website under his contact information. "Do you mind if I use the Hudson's landscaping and property to do the photography, Michael?"

"Be my guest," Michael said.

"You know, some Hudson's do community work. Maybe

your Hudson can adopt Patrick's vetery and do volunteer work to help him get started?"

"That's a brilliant idea, Bailey," Michael said.

The next morning, Bailey rushed to get dressed.

"Good morning!" Michael said, pulling her to him. He kissed her tenderly on the mouth.

"Hmm. Good morning," she said, holding onto him. "I like that. I can get used to being kissed each morning."

Once they reached the hotel, Michael found the doors unlocked. "They've returned," he said.

"I should hope so." She headed to the kitchen, with Michael beside her.

Bailey put on her apron and rolled up her sleeves. She pulled the menu out of the cabinet and then pulled out the pans she would use. After getting the bacon set out on the cookie sheet, she loaded it into the oven. Then she prepared the eggs for omelets. She had to cook them individually and place them in the oven to keep warm. Michael helped her get that part done. While the bacon was cooking, she placed another cookie sheet with bread on it, into the oven.

She got the coffee pot ready. While things were cooking, she gathered the plates and plastic ware she would need. She quickly picked up the routine and got breakfast under way, while she and Michael talked about foods they liked to eat.

"I should have brought a notebook," she said.

"I'll fetch your notebook from the car, love," he said. He left the kitchen, while she kept watch on the food. She would need to jot down notes to remember to tell the new hires while they are training.

He quickly returned and handed her the notebook and a pen.

"Thank you, Michael." She made her notes about the routine and the process for cooking. When the coffee was ready, he took it to the meeting room, along with the cups and condiments. She made more notes about the setup of the breakfast area for when that room was completed.

Breakfast was ready to go with five minutes to spare. Michael helped her bring it out to the meeting room. Larry walked into the room, followed by Maria, Ted, and Dave.

They all sat together and ate, while Maria filled Bailey in on their journey back to Shannon.

When they finished their meal, Michael helped Bailey with the clean-up.

"Tonight, either you or Larry gets to cook for us," she said.

"I guess I can take my turn. Did you get the burgers?"

"Yes, I believe so."

He kissed her forehead. "If you need anything, I'll be up on the second floor, working with the plumbers."

She watched him walk away. She liked everything about him so far. She poured herself a cup of coffee and headed back into the kitchen. She took the hamburger meat out of the freezer to thaw and then headed to the meeting room.

The new hires had arrived and Patrick had them all watch the Hudsonality video. After sitting through it, she remembered why she liked working at the Hudson Inn. Even though each team member may have a different job, the overall goal was to make the guest feel at home and help them to have a great time while they stayed at the Hudson Inn. She enjoyed being able to make people feel at home. She liked being needed.

Patrick approached her while everyone sat at a computer to start on their training.

"I'll go over the hands on training in the kitchen today, Bailey, if you want to help the front desk staff with any questions they may have," he said.

"I'll be glad to," she said. "Oh, and I have the hamburger sitting in the sink, thawing out for our dinner tonight."

"Duly noted," he said. Patrick led three women into the kitchen area for their training.

Bailey stood by the computers being used for the front desk personnel, while Maria took a crew upstairs to show them how to make a bed, Hudson style, using Linda's room as a training ground. She would also teach them how to clean everything else according to Hudson standards. When they were through with that training, Dave would have his own room.

Ted was busy helping Larry or Michael, since his expertise was in maintenance.

Around noon, all the new hires took a one-hour break. Ted made the peanut butter sandwiches, while the old crew sat together and ate, talking about how everyone was doing. This time, Patrick joined them.

"I should be getting in the equipment this week for the kitchen," Patrick said. "Once it's in place, I'll have the girls prepare breakfast for everyone. I've also placed a food order. I want them to learn how to inventory the orders when they come in and date everything."

"I guess I could make a list of Michael's items today, so I know what to pack up when the new equipment arrives," she said.

"Brilliant," Patrick said. "I'll let you know when it comes in."

"I'll be cooking tonight on the grill if it doesn't rain," Michael said.

"And if it does rain?" Larry asked.

"I'll be cooking with the oven."

When everyone returned from the lunch break, Bailey continued with the front desk staff. Luckily, they didn't have many questions.

Maria continued with her training. Each person had to prove to her they could make a bed, strip a bed, clean the bathroom and the room, doing it quickly. She timed them as well.

Dave gave assistance when there was a computer issue, but he could answer any question they had about front desk situations as well. Bailey wondered if she was needed at all at this stage. Once they had to deal with a real front desk, she would be more helpful.

Patrick called it a day after three hours in the afternoon. In total, the new hires all worked about six hours and went home. Patrick headed to his office. "I'll be doing some ordering before heading home. Bailey, you have tomorrow morning off from cooking breakfast."

"Thank you!" she said. Bailey headed to her room to work on her story, while Michael and Larry continued to work with the contractor and plumbers.

Finally, there was a knock on her door.

"Michael, are you needing help with dinner?" she asked when she saw him standing in her doorway.

"I would love your company, Bailey."

"I would love your company as well." She closed her door and joined him in the walk downstairs.

Michael prepared the hamburgers with seasonings. Since it was raining, he put the burgers on a cookie sheet and set the oven to broil.

"Too bad we don't have a broiler pan," she said.

"Oh, but I do have one." He pulled out his phone and called his son. "I need you to bring me the broiler pan, Patrick. Thank you. Oh, and a bottle of wine."

"Nice touch," she said.

Michael pulled the pan out of the oven, setting it on the counter. He prepared some French fries on another cookie sheet and placed them in the oven to bake.

"What would you like me to do?" she asked.

"We could slice up some tomatoes and lettuce," he said.

She pulled the tomatoes off the counter and the lettuce from the fridge, while Michael retrieved the cutting board and butcher knife.

"Michael, does Patrick have a way to get here besides his bicycle?" she asked.

"Yes, he has a car. He prefers riding his bicycle since everything is so close."

Moments after the tomatoes and lettuce sat on a plate, Patrick walked in with the items Michael requested.

Patrick opened the wine while Michael placed the burgers on the broiler pan and then in the oven.

"*Slainte*!" Patrick toasted Michael and then Bailey with paper cups.

"*Slainte*!" they said in unison.

"Have you eaten, yet, Patrick?" Bailey asked.

"No."

"Well, you'll have to join us, then," she said.

"Thank you. I think I will."

"While everything is cooking, Michael, I'm going to find some paper and make an inventory of your things so we'll be sure to return them when the other stuff comes in," she said.

Bailey left the kitchen and headed to the meeting room.

She found a sheet of paper and a pen and headed back to the kitchen, running into Patrick half way.

"Listen, Bailey, I'm sorry if I was rude the other day. My dad has been alone for two years and I worry about him. I can see you're making him happy and for that, I'm thankful."

"I totally understand. I have two sons and a daughter and they all worried about me traveling alone. I get it. I'm glad he has someone to worry over him."

She left Patrick and headed to the kitchen.

"How's it going?" she asked Michael.

He pulled her to him. "It's going much better now that you're back."

"Did I miss something?"

"No. I just missed having you here, with me."

Patrick returned and helped them bring the food out to the meeting room. "You look happy today, Dad," Patrick said.

"I am happy." He winked at Bailey and she smiled.

"The builders will be breaking ground next week on the new clinic. I'll need to be there for that or you can go in my place, Patrick."

"Sure, sure. Let me know when and I'll be there."

After the dinner with her team members, Michael, Patrick, and Bailey helped clean up the kitchen and got everything ready for the next evening meal.

"Well, thank you for dinner, Dad. I'll be going now. It looks like the rain has let up."

"You didn't ride your bike, did you?" Bailey asked.

"No, no. I drove."

"See you later, son."

"I still have my things in your car, Michael," Bailey said.

"Well, then I guess we should go to my place." He offered his arm and she took it.

After Michael parked his car in his driveway, he realized there was another car there. Who could that be? A friend of Patrick's maybe?

He helped Bailey out of the car and retrieved her overnight bag from the trunk. He offered his arm and she took it, clutching her camera bag in the other hand.

Once inside, he came face to face with Fionnuala. Patrick had been trying to dismiss her, but she wasn't taking the hint.

"Well, there you are, Michael," she said. "And who is this?" she pointed to Bailey.

"This is Bailey Jackson. She was with me in Murphy's a few days ago." He wrapped his arm around her. And she reached her arm around his back.

"We have work to do, Michael. Don't you have someplace we can talk. Privately?" Fionnuala glanced down at Bailey.

"Right here, in my office, Fionnuala." He pointed down the hall toward the front door.

"Make yourself useful and go get us some wine, Bailey," Fionnuala said.

Bailey glanced up at Michael. "You'll not talk to Bailey like that Fionnuala."

"She's your help, isn't she?"

"No, she's not."

"Don't tell me she's the one mentioned in the papers?"

"Papers?" Bailey asked.

"I'll explain later, Bailey," he said. "Fionnuala, why don't you come back another time?"

Fionnuala glared at Michael. "I guess you don't want my help with your fundraiser, then?" She turned to leave.

"Wait! Fionnuala, I do need your help. Have a seat. I'll be right back."

"I'll show her to the office, Dad," Patrick said. He led Fionnuala to the office, while Michael led Bailey back toward the kitchen.

"I'm sorry Bailey. Fionnuala is one person I don't like meeting with alone. She twists things around and I don't trust her."

"But money talks, right?"

"Well, her father's money and friends is what I need but she came along for the ride." He reached up into a tall cabinet and pulled down a bottle of wine. Then he retrieved two wine glasses.

"What was Fionnuala talking about when she mentioned papers?" Bailey asked.

"Oh, it was your idea. Remember when you said my problem was, I was too eligible?"

"Yes!"

"Well, I put in an advert for the papers mentioning I was spoken for by someone from the States. Although I didn't mention any names."

"Great idea. Now maybe they will leave you alone."

"I hope so. Especially, Fionnuala. This meeting is to go over the logistics for the banquet. The Findleys own a catering company, along with the architecture firm."

She reached up and pulled him toward her and gave him a kiss. He pulled her closer and kissed her back.

"Hmm. Thank you, love," she said. She gave him a wink and he winked back.

Patrick came into the kitchen. "I don't like this."

"What do you mean?"

"Fionnuala. Her showing up at this hour can only mean trouble. Will you be staying the night?"

"Yes, but I don't know if I should wait in the living room or the bedroom," she said.

Patrick pulled out the Jameson and Bailey's and poured each of them a drink. "Let's go into the living room."

Bailey and Patrick sat in the living room, chatting and sipping their drinks. After about two hours, Patrick went to check on them.

10

LOST

Patrick opened the office door with his key when no one answered. The office was empty. It was half past ten. He knew Fionnuala had ulterior motives. She had been after his father since his mother died. The woman was a gold digger and if she thought someone had money, she wanted a piece of the action.

He called his dad's cell. There was no answer. That was not like him to not answer the phone. He walked the property and found a small scruffy-looking dog outside on the patio. The dog came straight to him and he squatted down to pet her. "Hey little one. Where did you come from?"

"I'm lost."

"You are, aren't you. Well, we'll see if we can find your family. You stay here for tonight. I'll check on you in the morning."

Patrick opened the garage. His dad's car was there, and so was his own car. He rarely drove it now that he was home from university. Fionnuala's car was gone, however.

"Damn!" He tried calling his dad's cell once more. No answer. *Where could he be?* He headed back inside the house.

Bailey stood up and walked toward him.

"I thought you went to the office," she said.

"He's not there and neither is Fionnuala. I walked around the property and saw her car was gone," he said.

"Oh, no!"

"I've called him twice and he doesn't answer."

"From the look on your face, I take it you're worried."

"Yes. Fionnuala is not to be trusted."

"Doesn't she live in Limerick?"

"Yes. I'll call Findley and see if he knows where his daughter is." He dialed the number and sat beside Bailey on the sofa.

"Hello? Findley, this is Patrick Shaunnessy. I was wondering if you knew where Fionnuala was?"

"She had some plans with Michael for the week." Findley said.

"Did she say where she was going?" Patrick asked.

"Dublin, I think."

"Dad didn't say anything to me about it. He has a project to run and can't be running off with Fionnuala on a whim. Can you reach her and have her call me, please?"

"I'll give it a try," he said.

Patrick glanced at Bailey. "I think my father's been kidnapped." Findley was no help. He never liked the man, but he couldn't tell his father that since Findley and Michael were business partners.

Bailey covered her mouth. "Oh my gosh!"

"He told you he was an angel, didn't he?" Patrick asked.

She nodded. "Are you telepathic?" she asked.

"I…don't know. I can hear animals' thoughts, but I've never tried with people."

"Well, if Michael can insert himself into dreams, is he telepathic?"

"Let me try something." Patrick concentrated on his dad. *"Dad, if you can hear me, let me know if you're all right."*

There was no response.

"I got nothing." Then he remembered the conversation from the day before. "Why don't you try. If you and Dad have a spiritual connection, maybe you can speak to him." Bailey was his only hope now.

She closed her eyes and thought of Michael. *"Michael, I'm here, in your beautiful home, waiting for you. Where are you, Michael? I miss you. Patrick and I are worried about you. Speak to me, Michael. Let me know where you are."*

"Hello, love. I'm in a hotel room, but I don't know where. My mind is fuzzy. Send Patrick."

"Send him where, Michael?"

She opened her eyes. "He answered me, Patrick. He said his mind is fuzzy. He wants me to send you but he didn't say where, except he's in a hotel room."

Patrick ran his hand through his hair. "A fuzzy mind could mean he was drugged." He stood and paced in the living room.

"I agree. He took wine into the office to share with Fionnuala," she said.

Patrick pulled out his phone. "I should call the Garda," he said. He glanced at her. "The police."

"Try calling your dad again."

He dialed him again, but there was no answer. "I wonder if Fionnuala has his phone."

"Why would she do this?" Bailey asked.

"She's been after him since my mum died."

"Hello love. I think I'm in Tullamore. Send Patrick with some clothes."

"Michael, love. We're on our way."

"He just spoke to me. He thinks he's in Tullamore. He said to send you with some clothes. I told him we are on our way."

Patrick reached a hand out to her and helped her off the sofa. "Tullamore is about mid-way to Dublin. If you go with me, you won't be back in time to work tomorrow."

"Okay. I understand. I'll just keep talking to him this way. What do you need me to do around here?"

"There's a stray dog outside who is lost. If you can find her some food and water, that would be grand." He wrote down some instructions. "Here's the key to my car so you can get back to the hotel. I'll drive Dad's car."

"Thank you. Be careful, Patrick. Call me when you find your dad and let me know that he's okay."

Patrick headed to his father's room and returned with some clothes in his hands. He went into the kitchen and retrieved a paper sack and stuffed the clothes in a bag and headed out the door.

Bailey grabbed her camera and headed out through the patio door. A small movement caught her eye. She walked around the flowers until she found what she was looking for. It was a small, scruffy-looking dog.

"What's your name, little one?" She checked for a collar, but she didn't have one. She scooped up the dog and found an outside faucet. "Hmm." She needed soap to give the dog a bath so she headed back inside. She found some clean, old rags in the kitchen and took some dish soap. She went outside and gave the dog a bath, drying it quickly.

"We need to find your family." She headed back inside, grabbed some leftover scones and brought them outside, giving some to the dog. Then she had an idea. She set the small dog in the flower beds, capturing the dog and roses together, using her flash. She gave the scones as treats when the dog sat still and discovered the little one was willing to cooperate for the scones. After several minutes, she got some good shots of the dog.

Now, all she needed was to print out some of the images and create flyers to hang around town to see if anyone claimed the dog. She found a bowl in the kitchen and filled it with water and set it out for the small dog. The dog lapped up the water. Then Bailey got an old towel from the kitchen and folded it so the dog had a bed. She set the bed in an area that was covered, so it wouldn't get wet.

Bailey locked the front door like Patrick showed her. She went and checked on the small dog once more, giving it some pieces of ham for the evening. Then she locked up the patio door and climbed into Patrick's car. After making adjustments to the seat and mirror, she headed down the road. It was weird, driving on the wrong side of the road, while sitting on the wrong side of the car. Once she parked at the hotel, she realized she left her overnight bag in Michael's car.

She headed upstairs and pulled out her computer. Using her skills, she turned the images into signs for a lost dog and saved the files so she could later have Michael print them out.

Then, she thought about doing flyers for the dog shots to help Patrick make money for his clinic. She then took several images and tweaked them with information underneath each one, offering to do pet photos for a donation of $25 to go toward the new clinic.

"I'm here, Michael, sitting on my bed, waiting for you. Patrick is on his way. He's bringing you some clothes."

"Hello love, I miss you. I'm sorry I've disappointed you."

"You haven't disappointed me, Michael. I'm just worried about you. Help is on the way."

She set her alarm and tried to sleep, but sleep escaped her. She tossed and turned all night, thinking of Michael.

By morning, she was up before the alarm went off. She hurriedly dressed and took her notebook downstairs to start her day. When she glanced at her phone, she realized she missed Patrick's call. She called him back. She walked out onto the side patio for privacy.

"Patrick! Is everything all right? Did you find your dad? Is he okay?"

"Yes, Bailey. I made it very early this morning. I didn't want to wake you, so I called when I thought you'd be up for breakfast. Dad's fine, but I had him checked at the hospital. They said he had been drugged. There were traces of something in his bloodstream, but it should be gone by later today. He's still a little fuzzy headed. Here, he wants to speak with you."

"Hello, love. I'm sorry I put you through this."

"Michael, I'm so glad you're all right. I miss you. We can talk when you feel up to it."

She headed to the kitchen out of habit and quickly realized the new breakfast crew had everything under control.

"We'll be serving breakfast in the new breakfast area," Patrick said.

"Wonderful. I'll tell the others," she said. Bailey headed into the meeting room, but no one was there yet.

Then she remembered the tiny dog on Michael's patio. She would save her some food and take it there before the front desk shift got started. She would have to put up the notice about finding the dog when Michael and Patrick got back.

She headed upstairs to work on her manuscript, while she waited for breakfast. She had been working for thirty minutes when her alarm went off on her phone. She headed downstairs and this time, found both the old crew and the new hires standing around in the meeting room.

"Breakfast will be served in the new breakfast area," she announced. She escorted everyone to that section. The lights were on and the food was set out in bowls and trays.

"Hopefully this week we'll have our chaffers and serving equipment," Patrick said.

Everyone helped themselves, while the breakfast hostesses refilled bowls or pitchers, or made coffee.

Shortly after everyone cleaned up after themselves, the new hires sat at the computers. Ted went to work with Larry, and Maria took her crew upstairs to practice once more on Linda's old room before turning it over to Dave.

"Have you seen Michael?" Larry asked her.

"No, but I heard from his son. He may not be in today. I have to return his car. I can find out for you then," she said.

"Please do. Otherwise, I'll have to work with the plumbers and the cabinet people," he said.

"I can help you there," Ted said.

She rushed to the kitchen for any scraps for the small dog and got a plastic bag with leftover eggs and some toast. She checked with Dave for covering for her and then headed to Michael's house. She had her camera with her. When she pulled up to his driveway, she was the only one there. She quickly left the scraps for the small dog, snapped more pictures with the daylight sun, and headed back to the car. Just as she got inside the car, Patrick pulled up in his dad's car.

She jumped out of the car and ran to Michael's side.

"Michael! Oh, love. Are you feeling all right? Can I get you anything?"

He grabbed her and hugged her to him. "I've missed you, Bailey. Let's go inside."

Patrick set a newspaper down on the bar. "Here's the advert about Michael Patrick Shaunnessy being engaged to a woman from the States," he said.

"I've missed you, Michael." She glanced at the short article, which basically had what she suggested to him the day they were in Mary's shop. Michael kept his arm around her.

"Here's today's paper," Patrick set another set of papers on top of the first.

"Socialite claims to be the woman engaged to Michael Patrick Shaunnessy." She read further. "Socialite, Fionnuala Findley claims to be the woman engaged to the most eligible bachelor, Michael Patrick Shaunnessy, of Roundstone." The worst part was seeing a picture of Michael and Fionnuala kissing.

"It looks like a selfie," she said.

"And dad doesn't look like he's awake."

"I don't remember anything after pouring a second glass of wine for both of us," he said.

"That wasn't even taken here. It looks like the hotel I found him in," Patrick said.

"Did she leave you there, naked?" She asked.

"No, he had his under garments on," Patrick said.

"That was thoughtful of her. Please tell me she means nothing to you, Michael."

"Bailey, you're the only woman I want in my life." He lifted her chin and kissed her. She clung to him. She wanted to believe that.

"Well, Dad. I do have to work today. Lucky for me, it's

the night shift. I'm going to bed for a few hours." Patrick headed to his bedroom.

"You're not mad at me?" Michael asked.

"Why would I be mad at you?"

"Because I let someone like Fionnuala take advantage of me."

"Michael, she's the one with the problem. I mean, you could press charges against her for kidnapping you, couldn't you?"

"Patrick said as much. If I do that, then the whole fundraiser is down the toilet."

"Hey, speaking of fundraisers, I need you to let me print out a few pictures of a found dog and then some with the ad for pet photos. I hope you don't mind if I use your garden as well as the hotel property to do the pet photos?"

"Not at all. Go right ahead. What's mine is yours," he said.

"Really, Michael? Thank you!" She kissed him and he returned the kiss. Before the kiss grew deeper, she stopped him.

"Larry wants to know if you're coming in today?"

"I'll make it a half day. I'm not my whole self. I couldn't even blink on any clothes."

"Will you be coming in this morning or this afternoon?" she asked.

"I guess this morning," he said. "Let me shower and shave and we'll head to the hotel together."

Bailey waited for him in the living room while he got ready.

By the time they arrived back at the hotel, Bailey told him about the little dog.

"I'll check on her when I get back," Michael said.

"Good. I'll have my flash drive ready with the flyer information this afternoon." She took his hand. "I'm so glad you're safe Michael. I didn't get much sleep worrying about you."

He caressed her cheek. "I'm sorry you had to go through that, love. But it warms my heart that you cared that much about me."

"Michael, I love you. I don't want anything to happen to you."

He leaned in and kissed her, cradling her face in his hands. "Let's get back to work, then, shall we?"

She had confessed her love to him, but he didn't reciprocate. She let it slide. He called her love, that should count, shouldn't it? Besides, her husband never told her he loved her. Was that a guy thing?

She headed for the front desk staff and checked on their progress, while Michael headed upstairs to work with the plumbers.

During the remainder of the day, vendors came in with equipment for the kitchen. Patrick had the girls inventory everything and put the equipment up. They even brought Michael's things in the containers he had brought everything in. Bailey put them in the meeting room because it could be locked at night. She didn't see Michael again the rest of the day. When she went to her room, she found her suitcase sitting in front of her door.

It was Larry's night to cook and she realized she didn't take anything out for him. She headed back to the kitchen and found Larry standing in the center of the room, his hands on his hips. He turned when she entered.

"I guess, I forgot to take out the chicken," he said.

"I forgot too. Since the new kitchen hostesses prepared breakfast, I didn't even come in here."

"Tell everyone we're going to O'Donnel's and tonight we make our new list for this week," he said.

Bailey headed back to the meeting room. She found the old crew there, but the new hires had gone home. Once she told everyone about O'Donnel's, they headed back to their rooms to freshen up.

A sadness grew over her when they all arrived at O'Donnel's and Michael wasn't with them. It felt odd. She sat next to Maria and tried to carry on a conversation, but she was distracted.

"I heard we're getting the dressers in later this week," Maria said.

"When are the beds coming in?" she asked.

"I think the week after," Maria said.

"It seems like everything is finally coming together, just slowly," Bailey said.

"Hopefully, we'll finish the second floor cabinets and tubs this week," Ted said.

Everyone placed their orders and while waiting for their meals, enjoyed a beverage of some sort. She had a Smithwick's and enjoyed the flavor. It brought back memories of her and Michael's meal in the pub the other day. She hoped he was all right. Larry hadn't talked about him since early morning, and she didn't want to bring up the subject.

After about an hour or so, and creating the grocery list, the group headed back to the hotel. Tonight, she would get some writing done, since she hadn't heard from Michael. Maybe those drugs really affected him. He had said he felt fuzzy headed earlier.

Bailey worked on the manuscript for a couple more hours,

then decided to turn in. The lack of sleep finally took its toll. She didn't know if the breakfast hostesses would be fixing breakfast again, so she set her alarm for 7 a.m. When she lay down, she called out to Michael, like she had done so many nights before. *"I'm here, Michael. I miss your warm hugs and kisses."*

But this time, there was no answer.

11

CONFRONTATIONS

T he next morning, Bailey got up early and headed downstairs. Patrick, the GM was in the kitchen again with the three breakfast hostesses.

"Oh, you're cooking again?"

"Yes, we'll be doing this every day from here on out. Once we are open, we'll be serving breakfast at 6 a.m."

"It looks like you got your food order in," she said.

"Yes. We're going over how to process each order."

"I'll check back later, after breakfast. I need to take out some chicken for our dinner tonight," she said.

"That's fine," Patrick said.

Bailey headed back to her room and worked on her manuscript, while she waited for breakfast. Just before heading downstairs, she remembered to save her images for the flyers onto her flash drive, and put it in her pocket.

She headed to the breakfast area and got some coffee.

Before she could get to the meeting room, she ran into

Michael. She wasn't sure how to react, since he didn't respond to her the night before.

"Hello, Michael," she said.

He pulled her toward him and kissed her. "Hello, love. I'm sorry about last night. I took some medicine to help me recover from the drugs Fionnuala used and it knocked me out. I heard your voice, but I couldn't make the words come out. Can you forgive me?"

"Oh, Michael, of course I forgive you. I'm glad you're all right." She hugged him.

Out of the corner of her eye, she saw Larry heading toward the coffee.

"Is breakfast out yet?" he asked.

"No. Just the coffee. It should be any minute now," she said.

Then, the women came out with the chaffer trays full of food. Michael, Bailey, and Larry stepped away so they could work. Within minutes, the rest of the crew showed up and everyone helped themselves.

Patrick joined them. "Everything seems to be coming along in the kitchen area," he said.

"That's grand," Michael said. "We should have the bathrooms completed by next week and the beds will arrive shortly after that."

"The computer training should be completed by the time the beds come in," Bailey said. "Any word on the front desk?" She glanced at Michael.

"They are bringing in the dressers later this week, so that's about when we'll see the front desk," Michael said.

"I heard from the laundry people," Patrick said. "They will be installing the washers and dryers by the end of this week."

"Well, this is moving along great. Bailey and I will be

doing the grocery shopping tonight for the rest of this week," Larry said.

"Ah, you'll be needing the card again," Michael said. He reached into his back pocket and pulled out his wallet. He handed Larry the card.

Bailey waited until she was alone again with Michael and told him she had the flash drive with the flyer information on it.

"When you finish your shopping, I'll bring you to the house so we can print out the flyers."

"I'm looking forward to it," she said.

The rest of the day was uneventful, but Bailey felt better about what had happened the day before. She brushed away the feelings of doubt that had crept into her thinking.

After dinner, Michael gave her hand a squeeze since they couldn't be alone. "Text me when you get back tonight," he whispered. Then he left for home. Bailey went with Larry to the grocery store and finished the weekly shopping.

When they got back, Larry helped her with the first few bags, then disappeared. Just like he did to Linda. She finished putting everything away and then texted Michael.

He came within eight minutes.

"Wow, that was fast," she said.

"Pack a bag, I'm keeping you with me tonight," he said.

Once she arrived at Michael's house, she spent some time with their new visitor, the small dog, before printing her flyers. Afterward, Michael made all her doubts fade away. He pampered her with kisses after they enjoyed a leisurely time in the bath. She fell asleep in his arms, feeling loved.

The next morning, the two of them headed back to the hotel, where Bailey worked with the front desk staff and Michael supervised the plumbers.

It was Maria's turn to cook, so Bailey took the flyers she and Michael had printed out the night before, and she put them up in the shops in Roundstone. She got the word out about her photographic endeavors for Patrick's new clinic. The people she talked to seemed excited to have a Vet clinic in Roundstone.

She had no luck finding the owner of the small dog. She also discovered there was no place in town that printed images. She would have to see if Michael knew of a place in another town. When all the flyers were out, she walked back to the hotel.

Michael had gone home to take care of the small dog and promised to return for her.

By the time Bailey got back to the hotel, the meal was ready but Michael hadn't returned. She ate with the others.

When the dinner was over, Bailey texted Michael but he didn't return the text. Then she texted Patrick to see if he knew anything. He returned her text saying he would be off in an hour. She grabbed her camera bag and phone and headed to Michael's on foot. It wasn't much further past the shops. She walked as fast as she could. Something could be very wrong, but she hoped not.

By the time she arrived at his home, she was exhausted. She climbed the few steps when several people burst through the front door as if leaving. A couple of them had cameras. Once she was inside, she found Michael at his desk.

"You look frazzled. What happened? she asked.

"Oh love, it was the newspapers."

"Really? What happened? What did they want?"

"They wanted details of my upcoming wedding."

Her heart skipped a beat. "What wedding?"

"The wedding to Fionnuala."

"I thought she didn't mean anything to you," she said. Her heart pounded now.

He stood and moved toward her. "She doesn't." He took her arms and pulled her toward him, hugging her fiercely.

"Did you tell them that?"

"Not exactly."

"What did you say to them?" She pulled slightly away.

"I don't know. It happened so fast. I...believe I said they were mistaken."

"Mistaken about what?"

He rubbed his face. "I don't remember. I froze up. They all spoke at once." He turned her to face him. "Bailey, I'm not good at confrontations like that."

"Oh, Michael. This could be bad."

Patrick stepped into the office. "What could be bad?"

Michael turned toward Patrick. "The newspapers were here today."

"You didn't speak to them, Dad?"

"Well, yes, I did."

"What did you say?" Patrick asked.

Michael ran a hand through his hair. "I really don't remember."

"I think you should let me handle them from here on out, Dad."

"Yes, son, that's a brilliant idea."

Patrick glanced at Bailey. "How did you get here?"

"I walked. Fast."

"You walked here from the hotel?" Michael asked.

"Yes. I was worried about you. You didn't answer my text."

"We will have to make sure he isn't alone with Fionnuala," Patrick said.

"Definitely."

"If she calls you, Dad, you make sure she comes here and Bailey or I will be with you."

"Sure, sure. That will be grand."

"Have you two eaten dinner yet?" Bailey asked.

"No," Michael said.

"Me neither," Patrick said.

"Well, let me see what you have in the fridge and I'll fix something for you," Bailey said.

Bailey left with Patrick and headed to the kitchen.

"How long has your dad had this aversion to confrontations?" she asked.

"All my life, I'm afraid. Mum was hard to live with. Very demanding at times. I didn't realize he was always giving in and doing things for her to make her happy until my teens. But that's when I realized that no matter how hard he tried, she was never really happy."

"There's always hope," she said.

"In Dad's case, I don't know."

"My husband was like your mother. Nothing made him happy. He would find things to argue about. I think it's made me a stronger person, but not when he was around."

"I can see you're already making dad happy, Bailey. Maybe with your help, he can overcome his problem."

"I hope so." Bailey busied herself in the kitchen and got everything ready for dinner. "I put up signs today about the little dog. No one seems to know anything about her," she said.

"I guess we'll have to name her and bring her inside," Patrick said. "I'll have a talk with her later."

Michael walked in carrying something in his arms.

"Look who wanted to join us," he said.

"Ah, there she is. How are you girl?" Patrick said. The dog waged her tail and licked Patrick when he picked her up. "She loves your scones, Bailey," he said.

"Really? They were in your fridge. I need to feed her more than that," she said.

"How did she get here?" Michael asked.

"I found her in the flower garden, all dirty," Patrick said.

"I set out a couple bowls with water and some food after I bathed her, when Patrick went to find you," Bailey said. "She's been on the patio since then."

"Maybe we should wait a bit before naming her in case someone claims her," Michael said.

Michael gave the dog a pat on the head.

"Her name is Daisy," Patrick announced.

"Well, that settles it then," Bailey said.

"You two can fix her a bed in here and we'll take turns walking her in the garden," Patrick said.

"Brilliant," Michael said.

Michael took the old newspapers and placed them on the bathroom floor. Bailey found some old rags and fixed a bed in the bathroom, away from the papers.

"You'll be all right for a little bit, won't you, girl?" Bailey asked. She closed the door to the bathroom and went back to the kitchen to fix Michael a portion of the leftovers. When she got there, he had helped himself and sat at the bar.

"I would have gotten you something, Michael."

"I know, love. I'm not helpless and I don't want you to feel you have to wait on me."

She put her hand on his back. "I don't mind, really."

"You're spoiling me, love. I'd rather spoil you."

"Well, I'm enjoying all your attention." She sat beside him. "I'd like to know what you like to eat so I can fix it for you," she said.

"I'll eat anything you fix, love. No complaints here."

"Michael, is there any place nearby that will print pictures?"

"In Galway, there's a place."

"Is it walking distance from here?"

"No, love. I'll take you to Galway. When do you need to go?"

"Oh, that would be great. Once I'm finished with the photography, I'll need to make prints of everything."

Fionnuala sat at the bar in O'Malley's, nursing a Guinness.

"Mr. Shaunnessy was vague about the details, can you give us a date for the wedding?" the reporter asked.

"It'll be next spring. We haven't worked out the details," she said.

"How did he propose?"

"We had a nice meal in Tullamore and he proposed in the restaurant," she said.

"Did he give you a ring, then?"

"No, no. We'll be picking one out after the fundraiser for his son, Patrick's vetery."

"His son has a vetery?"

"He will have one by the end of the year. I'm planning the fundraiser for this month. It's a big affair with $1,000 plate dinners to raise funds for his equipment."

"Lovely, lovely. Now, where is this wedding going to be held?"

"It'll be on the west coast of Ireland. I'll have more information for you after the fundraiser."

"Thanks a million. I'll be in touch."

On Saturday, Bailey and Michael headed for Galway after breakfast.

"So, what do you do in your spare time besides painting, Michael?" she asked.

"My spare time?"

"Yes, when you aren't consumed with the hotel."

"Well, I usually design homes or office buildings for others at the firm in Limerick. When I have time, besides painting, I like to watch football or read a good book. I would love to go dancing sometime. Megan would never do that with me."

"You need to finish that picture you started last week."

"Yes. Maybe tomorrow, if it isn't raining, we can go back and do that for a bit."

"I'd love that," she said.

She located a drug store that printed images from a flash drive. She had one with her, so she wouldn't have to purchase one. While she found her information, Michael shopped for Daisy. When the two met up, he had a basket full of items for the dog.

"You went all out, didn't you?"

When they returned home, the two of them walked Daisy in the garden with her new leash and collar. Bailey had brought her tripod with her and set it up. She took images of Michael and Daisy. Then she set her timer and sat next to Michael. He put his arm around her and she grabbed his hand, placing it in her other hand in her lap when the shot went off. Luckily, both of them were smiling.

When they headed inside, Michael pulled out a large portfolio of paintings, hidden in the back of the closet, and opened them on the bed.

"Michael, these are beautiful. You should hang them here in your residence and in the hotel for your guests to enjoy."

"You think so?"

"Yes! You can even make prints of them and sell them to the guests."

"How would I do that?"

"Well, I can photograph them and take them to the printers in Galway. We can make them any size and have them printed on canvas. I can make small signs to put with each original, saying prints available for purchase upon request."

"These are all big prints," he said.

"We can have them printed smaller if you want. You can decide what size and what price."

"I like that idea. I'll think on it."

She helped him put his paintings away.

"Let's go to O'Donnel's and have a meal tonight," he said.

"Oh, I'd like that."

After getting Daisy situated in the bathroom once more, Bailey and Michael headed out. O'Donnel's was walking distance from his home and it wasn't raining.

Once inside, they sat at the bar.

"Dad! What are you doing here?" Patrick asked.

"We've come to eat. Have you got any food?"

"Of course, dad. What'll you have to drink?"

"Well, I'll have a Guinness. Bailey, what will you have?"

"I guess I'll have a Guinness, too."

"Be right back," Patrick said.

"The only thing I don't like about a Guinness is waiting for the foam to settle," she said.

After Patrick brought their drinks, they ordered a couple of steak dinners.

"Is it ready, yet?" Bailey asked.

"Not yet. Tell me what you do in your spare time, Bailey."

"There's not much spare time since I work two jobs. You know what I do at the hotel, working at the front desk. And I mentioned some things I do at the Brewery. If I have time, I write or work in my flower gardens. I photograph my flowers or scenics from where I live. Pulling weeds is something I hate doing, but it seems like that's what I do the most."

"Have you got any books with you?"

"No, but I'm working on one now. You should be able to find them in bookstores and online. Is the Guinness ready yet?"

"Not yet."

Patrick talked to a pretty red-head with beautiful blue eyes. Whatever he said to her made her blush. She approached them and brought them water.

"Thank you," she said.

The girl smiled and left.

"I think Patrick likes her," she said.

"What makes you say that?"

"The way he looks at her when she's around him."

Michael glanced over at the red head. "He's not

mentioned her before." He glanced at his drink. "The Guinness is ready."

He touched her glass as she picked it up. "What should we toast this time?" he asked.

"How about 'to happily-ever-afters'?" she asked.

"To happily-ever-afters."

Patrick approached the table. "Two steak dinners," he said.

"This looks yummy," she said.

Bailey and Michael chatted about different beers and silly things that happened at bars during their meal. She realized the few times she ate out with her husband, they had little to say to each other. She enjoyed the chit chat with Michael.

After dinner, they walked back to his home, making a stop in a local bookstore.

"I'd like to purchase a book by Bailey Jackson," he said to the shopkeeper.

The shopkeeper glanced through his inventory list. "I don't have any in stock, but I can order one for you."

"That'll be grand. Why don't you order copies of all of her books and I'll have the author sign them for you," he said.

"You know the author?"

"She's standing right here," Michael said.

"You're Bailey Jackson?" the shopkeeper asked.

"Yes, I am."

"Oh, goodness. Would you be available to sign the books next week?" the shopkeeper asked.

Bailey glanced at Michael, her brows raised. "I think so."

"I can advertise and have a book party."

"I love that idea. Let me know when and I'll be here," Bailey said.

"Make sure it's a Saturday," Michael added.

"Ah, yes. I am busy during the week," she said. She had almost forgotten she was working.

"Are you staying in town Ms. Jackson?"

"I sure am. I'm staying at the new Hudson Inn in Roundstone."

She pulled her author business card out of her camera bag. "Here's my card." It had her U.S. phone number on it.

Michael reached for the card and wrote his number on it. "You can reach her locally at this number."

"Brilliant! I will contact you as soon as the books are in."

After leaving the shop, she wrapped her arm through his. "Thank you, Michael. That will help my sales."

"My pleasure, love."

12

FINISHING TOUCHES

Bailey stayed busy the rest of that week and the following week. She booked appointments for the pet photos for late afternoons, mostly at the hotel. If they needed a Saturday, she booked them for Michael's place. Sometimes she did two and other times as many as six. She worked as quickly as she could and used some of Daisy's pet treats to entice some good shots. What surprised her was the fact the people ordered more than one image of their pets. In those cases, she gave a discount and gave them an option of 5x7s for the second print and an 8x10 for the first.

Before the first week was over, the shopkeeper called and scheduled the book party. She continued to make appointments for all the other days.

Patrick, the GM, covered for Michael a couple days when Michael was tied up with the contractors at his son's new clinic site. But when the book party date arrived, Michael escorted Bailey to the shop.

"I'm a little excited," she said.

"Me, too. I've never escorted an author before."

A table was set up in the front of the shop with Bailey's books. Some were stacked and some were displayed in front of the stacks. She sat at a chair, ready to sign books.

Michael stood before her. "I'd like one of each of your books, signed by you."

"Really?" She felt her face grow hot. What would she write besides her name? She usually put a note in each book to personalize it for the reader. She hesitated, then wrote: 'To my dream lover,' and signed Bailey. Then each consecutive one had a different message, sometimes using Michael and some with 'my love.' By the time she finished signing his books, people had gathered around.

The shopkeeper was busy telling people what was going on and ringing up sales. For the next two and a half hours, she signed books and talked to the readers. She enjoyed the enthusiasm of the readers and being able to connect with them.

When the last book was signed, the shopkeeper approached her.

"Thanks a million Ms. Jackson. I've seen a lot of sales today. I've almost sold out, thanks to you."

"Thank you, Art," she read his name tag. "This is how I earn money, too."

"When is your next book coming out?"

"I'm working on one right now. It takes place here in Ireland."

"Oh, that's grand. I would love to do another book party when it's ready."

"That sounds wonderful." She got his mailing address and email so she could contact him when the graphics and book cover were ready. Afterward, Michael walked her back to his house. When they got there, Michael set her books on the coffee table and began reading her first one, while she worked on her manuscript in the living room.

When Patrick came in, he tossed the newspaper on the coffee table.

Michael glanced up at him.

"You might want to read the headlines, dad."

"Ireland's Most Eligible Bachelor is Off Limits."

The article went on to say, 'Prominent businessman and architect, Michael Patrick Shaunnessy, is set to wed socialite, Fionnuala Findley next spring. The wedding will be held on the west coast. When asked for details, Shaunnessy was flustered and replied "Ask Fionnuala." The two will honeymoon in Europe.

When Michael put the paper down, Patrick commented. "You might want to call the papers and have that retracted, dad."

Michael stood and wrung his hands. "Easier said, Patrick."

He paced across the living room.

"It's all my fault, Michael," Bailey said.

"How is it your fault?" Patrick asked.

"I suggested he put an ad in the paper telling people he was not available," she said. "That was so the women would leave him alone."

"You didn't turn this into a circus like Fionnuala did," Patrick said.

"My ad said I was engaged to someone from the States. Fionnuala turned it around and claimed it was her," Michael said.

"Can you print a retraction?" Bailey asked.

"Or maybe you can call the papers and say you broke off your engagement," Patrick said.

"And have her pull out from this fundraiser? I think I'll

wait until the fundraiser is over. I need those people she knows to help us with funding," Michael said.

"Next week, I'll have to be at the site to supervise the foundation," Michael said. "I'll also have to be at the hotel and supervise the installation of the beds."

"Why don't you let Ted and Larry deal with that, Michael? Ted does that sort of thing all the time at our Hudson in the States," Bailey said.

"I can help you with the foundation, dad, if you prefer to be at the hotel," Patrick said. "Just tell me what to do."

"They will be pouring concrete early," Michael said.

"I'll help on those days, dad, they have me working a split shift for two weeks."

"Let me think on it, son," he said.

Bailey finished her week out, doing more pet shots. She scheduled more the next week so she could help Patrick raise funds for his equipment. She found time to send an email to Dee at the Smoky Brewery, letting her know what was happening in Ireland. Then she emailed all her children, telling them about Michael with a little more detail.

She realized the new hires would be ready to work the front desk and make reservations for the new Hudson once the desk was installed. One of these new people would become a supervisor of the others, so her training would be helpful to them. Her time at this Hudson would soon be coming to an end. Maybe two more weeks and the hotel would be ready to open officially, if not sooner.

That would mean she would be leaving Michael. Could she leave him now? Was there a future for both of them? Even Patrick was growing on her. She decided not to say anything to Michael just yet, especially since he would be needed on the site of the new clinic. He didn't need to worry about her feelings. This must be stressful for him with two projects going at one time.

She would finish what she started with the pet photos to help Patrick. Besides, she would work on her manuscript if she could carve out enough time. If Michael brought up the subject about their future, she would deal with it then. If he didn't want her in his future, then she would look at this as her 'Irish fling.' For now, she would enjoy his company.

It worked out that on weekends, Bailey stayed with Michael at his home. After breakfast on Saturday, Michael sat next to her on the patio, while they finished their coffee. They watched Daisy explore the garden.

"I don't have anything planned today, love. How about you?" Michael asked.

"I have a couple appointments this morning and then I'm free the rest of the day," she said.

"I thought I'd take you for a drive along the coast. The scenery is beautiful there. You can shoot pictures and I can paint."

"I love that idea. I'll pack a lunch for us," she said.

After her last appointment, she hurriedly put her things away while her camera battery was charging. She headed to the kitchen to pack a lunch, but Michael came in to help her.

"This is more fun when we do this together," she said.

"'Tis."

When they finished, she headed to the bedroom to retrieve her camera battery and lenses she might need. Michael gathered his painting supplies and loaded the car.

"Don't forget your easel," she reminded him.

"Thank you love. And did you pack a blanket?"

"No. I didn't know which one you'd prefer."

Michael went back inside and pulled a blanket off the shelf in his closet and grabbed his easel.

He finished packing the car and opened her door for her before getting in the car himself.

The drive was nice and Michael seemed relaxed. "I am so glad you enjoy doing this with me, Bailey." He took her hand and held it as he drove.

"I enjoy the scenery and getting to know Ireland more," she said. "But all this beauty needs to be shared. It wouldn't be as much fun if I did it by myself." She gave his hand a squeeze.

"So you had to sneak away the time for your passion, just like I did," she said.

He glanced at her. "Yes, I guess I did."

"That's how I had to write. I couldn't do it at home while my husband was there. He would just criticize me or insult me for wasting my time."

Michael pulled her hand up to his lips and kissed it. "You won't hear me complain about your writing time."

"And I won't complain about your painting."

When they got to their destination, Michael helped her set up the blanket and the food and drinks. Then he set up his easel and supplies. He got his canvas out and set it on the easel.

"I want to sketch you," he said.

"Me? I've never been sketched before. How do you want me?" she asked.

He took her hand and walked her to the blanket. "Have a seat there," he said. He pointed to a spot. After she sat down, he moved her legs and arms the way he wanted them. Then he tussled her hair and walked to the easel.

She sat there for several long minutes, trying not to move while he worked on the canvas. "You're doing great, Bailey. Just a few more minutes." When he finally let her take a break, she grabbed her camera and shot some pictures of him, working on his canvas.

The two of them sat on the blanket and had their lunch before he let her see what he had drawn.

"I like it so far, Michael. What did you do with the other one?"

"I will finish them both at home, wait 'til you see them."

He went back to work for a couple hours, while she photographed flowers and the scenery around them.

"I think that's enough for today. I'll work on it more tomorrow."

"Are we coming back here tomorrow?"

"No, I'll set it up on the patio and paint there. That way, there won't be any paint fumes in the house."

"Now that Megan is gone, you could set up a studio in your home, couldn't you?"

"I thought about that, but I don't know where I'd put a studio."

"Do you have a room you don't use? Or a building?"

"One day, Patrick will move out and be on his own. That day, I'll use his room for a studio."

"Oh, that's a good idea. I turned a bedroom into a sewing room when my daughter moved out."

They packed up their things in the car and headed back to the house.

"I really enjoyed today, Michael. Thank you for bringing me here. I love picnicking with you."

"Me, too, love, I mean with you."

The next week was busy for all of them. Patrick did his split shifts after spending time at the construction site with Michael, learning what needed to be done. Michael was busy at the building site, while Patrick, the GM, took care of things at the hotel. Bailey showed everyone the routines for each shift and volunteered to help train each person on their shifts, once Patrick made up the schedule and the desk was set up with phone lines and internet connections.

For a few days, she didn't get to see Michael when it was time to train the night auditor. She slept the next two days so she could stay awake for that shift. She brought her laptop with her and worked on her manuscript in between supervising the agents making reservations and doing the audit. By the time all three shifts went through their training, a week had gone by.

In between the shifts, she still did some pet portraits. She got all her images onto the flash drive and asked Michael if he could take her to Galway to have the images printed. Since the banquet was scheduled for the next week, she wanted to have the money in time for Patrick's event.

She had Michael decide on the sizes of prints he wanted to sell and the price, then she photographed all his images and put them on the flash drive with all the pet images. Then, one afternoon, she and Michael went to Galway. They were told that Michael's canvas prints would take longer, but her images could be done in a couple of hours.

She and Michael visited a museum while in Galway and

had a nice dinner at a local pub. Michael told her a little of the history of Galway, which made the whole day seem special.

"How will you pay for your images, Bailey?" he asked.

"Oh, I've been collecting money for all of the pet shots. I have enough to cover these and the rest will go to Patrick for his clinic."

The drive home was pleasant as Michael talked about what had happened at the job site and how they were coming along with the foundation.

"You should document the building of his clinic with images, Michael. It will be historic, since you don't have a Veterinarian clinic yet."

"You're right. I'll start doing that the next time I go to the site."

"Tomorrow, the pet owners will stop by to pick up their photos in the afternoon. I thought they could meet me in the sitting room if that's all right?"

"Sure, sure. How much were you able to collect for Patrick?"

"Well, I think it's about $1,000. Most of the pet owners bought more than one image each. They knew it was for the clinic, so they seemed glad to help out. A lot of them referred their friends."

"I'd say you were very successful. Patrick must be happy about it."

"I haven't told Patrick how much I've collected. I wanted to give him the money at the banquet."

"That's a brilliant idea. He would love it."

Bailey set about sorting the images with the notes she made. While she was at the shop in Galway, she purchased a receipt book so each person could have a receipt, along with their order of prints. She also purchased some very large zip bags to place the orders in for each customer. Once everything was organized, she contacted each customer and set an approximate time for the next day.

As an afterthought, she placed one of her business cards in each order so they could contact her if there was a question or problem. Or, hopefully, another print order.

She realized there was a wonderful smell coming from the kitchen. When she went to investigate it, she found Michael, cooking dinner.

"Oh, I could have done that, Michael," she said.

"You were busy, and I wanted the chance to cook for you," he said.

"What are we having?"

"We're having fish and chips, tonight, love."

"Sounds good. I haven't had fish since I've been here."

While they ate, Bailey brought up the subject of winding down at the hotel.

"I love the new front desk, Michael. It's got more storage than the desk we have at our Hudson. Oh, and the Irish marble is beautiful."

"'Tis. I picked it out. There was only so much I could do to flavor the hotel with Irish touches."

"You can put your paintings in each of the rooms. Since you had a variety, I chose eight different images and had enough printed for each room. Once they are ready, you need to have them framed," she said.

"Oh? I forgot about that. Yes, I know a framer. When will they be finished?"

"Next week."

"All that's left is the bed linens, towels and the lobby furniture," Michael said.

"Yes. The IT people have come to retrieve the computers

from the meeting room. They should be done by Monday," she said.

"It's beginning to look more like a hotel now," he said.

"Yes, it is. I saw the pool, the other day. It's gorgeous."

"They will be bringing in the patio furniture and some plants for the pool area when they bring in the lobby furniture," he said.

"It's so exciting, seeing a new hotel opening up," she said. Then her heart gave a hitch. What will become of her and Michael? She let the conversation end at that. She hoped Michael would pick it up and say what she wanted to hear, but he didn't.

She let the thought go. She wouldn't dwell on it, but instead, she would enjoy Michael's presence and his attention.

Later that night, she enjoyed another leisurely and passionate bubble bath with Michael. She lay beside him, feeling loved and content. His arms wrapped around her, a leg draped over her hip. He drew her close and kissed her good night.

13

FUNDRAISER

J ust after breakfast at Michael's, Bailey started cleaning up the kitchen. Michael joined her in the cleanup.

"I always appreciate your help, Michael. What's the occasion?"

"Today is the fundraiser, love. We'll have to hurry off to Limerick as soon as we're finished."

"Am I going too?"

"Of course you are. I told Fionnuala that I was bringing a guest."

"Thank you, Michael." She reached up and kissed his cheek.

He wrapped her in his arms and gave her a proper kiss.

"Hmm, if this kiss progresses like all your other kisses, we will be late," she said.

"I can't get enough of you, Bailey."

"I think we're both making up for lost time." She took his hand and led him to the bedroom.

She hurriedly dressed in the bathroom. She decided to

wear the cute dress that Michael had popped on her after her first night with him. It was the dressiest thing she had.

Michael dressed in the closet. She put on some makeup and curled her hair for extra body. When she saw Michael decked out in a suit, she realized she was underdressed.

"Maybe I shouldn't go, Michael. I don't have anything suitable to wear for an occasion such as this."

"Nonsense! He blinked and she wore a black, sexy cocktail dress. "Well, I guess this will do nicely. Thank you, Michael." She grabbed her envelope for Patrick and a small handbag she brought for special occasions, and joined Michael at the door. But he hesitated and closed the door. "Maybe I should just keep you here for myself," he said. He pulled her into a hug and kissed her neck.

"Whoa, that will make us very late if you don't stop now," she said.

"Hmm. We'll continue this activity later this afternoon," he said.

"I'm looking forward to it, love."

Patrick was already waiting in the living room. "You two look good," he said. He stood as they entered the room. He, too, was decked out in a suit. "You two Shaunnessy men are gorgeous. I can't help feeling excited for you both," she said. She walked up to Patrick. "Patrick, this is for you," she said. Bailey handed him the envelope of money.

"What's this?"

"It's from all those pet photos I did. Most of them were dogs, of course, but everyone was willing to help. They love the idea of having a vetery here in Roundstone."

Patrick reached over and hugged her. "Thank you, Bailey, for all you do around here. I didn't expect all this."

"I know, but I enjoyed doing it. You can count it if you like. There's a $1,000 there."

"She worked on it for a couple weeks, Patrick. I'd say she was brilliant, but I'm biased." Michael smiled at her and it made her smile as well.

"Thank you, too, dad for this fundraiser. You've done a lot for me since I began at university. How can I ever repay you?" Patrick said.

"You can repay me by being the best vet out there and build your reputation on honesty and integrity."

Patrick hugged Michael. Bailey rushed back into the bedroom and grabbed her camera. She got a few candid shots of the two men talking together.

"Now, I need an official of you two, standing together," she said.

Michael put his arm around Patrick, but they were the same height, making it a little awkward.

"Thank you, both," she said.

Patrick took her camera and got a shot of her and Michael. Michael put his arms around her, standing behind her, and she rested her arms on his.

"Let me get one of you handing Patrick the envelope," Michael said.

She posed with Patrick and the envelope and then they headed out the door.

"Did you let Daisy out this morning, Patrick?" Michael asked.

"Yes, dad, since she's been sleeping in my room, it was easy."

On the drive to Limerick, Michael chatted about the progression of the clinic, but he didn't mention the hotel.

Everything was done at the hotel and the rooms had been booking up since the front desk had been in full swing two weeks prior. All the bookings were for the next week and beyond.

Larry had told them he was leaving on Monday and would give anyone that needed it, a ride to the airport. Ted and Maria had chimed in, but she had been hesitant. She had waited for Michael to say something and he hadn't yet. Dave was staying on to give any computer or software support for after their official first guests.

When Michael finished talking, Bailey decided to change the subject when he didn't mention the hotel.

"So, Patrick, when are you going to invite that cute, red-haired server to dinner?" She turned in her seat for his reaction.

Patrick blushed. "Amelia?"

"Is that her name?"

"She's the only red-haired server we have besides her brother, Dennis. Dennis is the relief bartender."

"Well, maybe you could bring her home one night for dinner. I'll be glad to cook something for the two of you."

Michael glanced in the rear-view mirror.

"I…I've never thought about asking her out. What made you think of her?"

"I saw the way you two looked at each other the night your dad and I were at O'Donnel's."

He sat silent for a few minutes. "I have walked her home a time or two."

"That's a start," Bailey said. She turned back to the front and smiled.

When they entered the banquet hall, a gentleman approached them. "Michael Shaunnessy?"

"That's me," Michael said.

"I have a few questions about the auction. Can you come with me?"

"Sure, sure." He gave her hand a quick squeeze. "I'll be right back, love."

"We're a little early," Patrick said.

"While I have you alone, Patrick, I wanted to mention that all your future clients are listed with their phone numbers and their donations inside the envelope, as well as their pet's name. That way, you can write them thank you notes when you have time."

Patrick hugged her. "I appreciate all your hard work, Bailey. You amaze me."

"You remind me so much of your father. I wish you all the success in the world, Patrick."

"Thank you, Bailey. I'll ask Amelia to dinner next week."

"Good thinking."

"Excuse me. Patrick Shaunnessy?" a gentleman asked.

Bailey turned to see two strangers standing together, one in a priest's cassock.

"I'm Patrick Shaunnessy. Hello, Father Ambrose."

"Father Ambrose is here to speak with Michael Shaunnessy and I'm here to ask your opinion on the seating," he said.

"Well, Michael Shaunnessy will be right back. How can I help?"

"Come this way," he said.

"I'll be right back, Bailey," Patrick said.

"Hello Father. I've lost two Shaunnessy men in the span of minutes."

"Hello Bailey. Are you and Michael getting on all right?"

"So far, yes Father." She touched his arm. "How did you know about me and Michael?"

"Michael and I have had several chats about his dream

over the past year. I take it you are the Bailey he spoke about."

"Yes, I guess I am."

"And have your dreams come true as well?"

"I don't know how much he told you, father, but most of them have played out. It was mostly how we met. It was always how we met, but in different places or situations. Since we met, I haven't had those dreams any more. So, maybe they were premonitions and not dreams."

"Michael said as much."

"Well, I was hoping Michael would make our relationship permanent."

"Ah, he's not stepping up to the plate. Where is Michael?"

"Someone came and got him like they did Patrick. I'm here, waiting." She heard the clicking of heels against the tile floor. She glanced over her shoulder and saw Fionnuala, dressed in a low-cut, black evening gown that highlighted her sexy figure.

"What are you doing here?" Fionnuala asked.

"We're both waiting for Michael Shaunnessy."

"Aren't you supposed to be in the kitchen?"

"No, I'm Michael's guest."

Fionnuala looked her over. "Michael's guest is Patrick. He said so, himself." She waved her hand in an exaggerated way before Bailey caught sight of the rock on her ring finger. "Besides, you aren't on the guest list. I'm sure you couldn't afford to be on the help's list, either." She cackled.

Bailey's pulse raced. What was happening? Where was Michael?

"Fionnuala, I'm here to speak to Michael. Can you get him for me?" Father Ambrose asked.

"Really Father? I'm not your messenger. I don't recall you being on the list either."

Bailey glanced at Father Ambrose. "I think there's been a misunderstanding here."

"You're right," Fionnuala said. She punched something in on her phone. "Unless you two leave right now, I'll have the Garda escort you out for trespassing." Fionnuala held the phone up, her hand poised to press the enter key.

Bailey clenched her jaw and fought back tears. "Father, can I have a lift?"

"Sure, sure." He turned and walked toward the door with Bailey at his side. She could hear Fionnuala's heels clicking against the tile. When she reached for the door, Fionnuala beat her to it. She held the door open for the two of them.

Bailey glanced at the rock-sized ring once more.

Fionnuala tucked her hair behind her ear. "Oh, didn't Michael tell you? We chose my ring the other day. Isn't it beautiful?" She held out her hand so the obvious ring couldn't be missed by even a blind man.

Bailey pushed through the door without another word. Once she was outside and the door closed between the red-head and herself, she spoke up.

"Well, now I know why Michael has been dragging his feet."

"I'm sorry Bailey. I had high hopes for the two of you and I've been praying this relationship would work." Father said.

"Thank you Father. I'll still be needing your prayers and a lift to the airport."

"Airport?"

"Michael won't be needing two women in his household after this evening."

"Sure, sure."

The ride from Limerick turned into a confessional as

Bailey bared her soul. She told him how her dreams had started and then ended when she and Michael became intimate. She felt comfortable around Michael, but now she was hurt. She went on to mention how Fionnuala had twisted his original ad in the papers to her advantage and even kidnapped him before putting out the article that they were engaged.

"Do you think Fionnuala lied to the news reporters?" he asked.

"Yes, I do, but Michael never made an attempt to correct the facts. He was worried that she wouldn't fulfill her obligation for this fundraiser for Patrick's vetery."

When they arrived at Michael's, Bailey found his spare key and let herself and Father Ambrose inside. She collected her things, packing quickly, while Father waited for her. She locked up then left the key where Michael had it originally. "I'll need a ride to the hotel to get the rest of my things, Father. If you don't mind." She pulled some money from her small handbag and gave it to the priest. "For gas," she said.

"No, no. I can't take it," he said.

"Then, it's a donation, Father."

He hesitated, then took the money.

When they arrived at the hotel, she ran into Larry.

She swallowed hard and forced back the tears. "I'm heading out today, Larry. I'll see you all back in the States."

Father Ambrose waited in the lobby while she packed her things, checking every drawer and outlet, making sure she had everything. She glanced around the room one last time. It had been her home for almost two months. She took a picture of the room before heading out the door.

The ride to the Shannon Airport had been a quiet one. She only hoped she could get a ticket back to the States without any problem.

The dinner gala began with announcements and introductions of high society attendees. The silent auction items were laid out on a long table for everyone to peruse while cocktails were served.

Michael glanced around the room, visually searching for Patrick and Bailey. He moved through the crowd trying to find them, with no luck. When the call went out to be seated, he found Patrick.

"Where's Bailey?"

"I left her in the lobby with Father Ambrose. I meant to go back, but I got held up. Didn't you go back for her?" Patrick asked.

"No, I got held up as well." He wrung his hands. "I don't like this." He turned toward the entrance to get Bailey, but felt an arm on his shoulder.

"Michael, are you leaving us?" Findley asked.

"I'm going to get my guest," Michael said.

"Everyone is here. Congratulations, by the way." Findley moved him around to face the tables.

"Thank you?" Michael had a sinking feeling something wasn't right.

Findley guided him to two empty seats. Findley took the one on the left and pulled out the one on the right for Michael.

He searched all the faces at the table and Bailey wasn't among them. To his right was Fionnuala.

"Where's Bailey?" he asked her.

"Who?"

"Bailey Jackson, my guest. I told you I was bringing a guest."

"Oh, Michael, there must be a misunderstanding. I thought Patrick was your guest."

"Patrick is the guest of honor. I made it clear that Bailey was my guest."

"I'm sorry." She pretended to look around the table. "I don't see her here. Perhaps she changed her mind."

"What have you done, Fionnuala?"

She touched his hand. "Michael, I've worked hard getting this fundraiser off the ground."

He glanced at her hand on his and didn't miss the large diamond.

"Whose ring is that?"

"Why, don't you remember? Our special night in Tullahome, where you proposed to me?" She waggled her fingers. "It's gorgeous, Michael. I love it." She moved to kiss his cheek, but he stood up.

"Excuse me." He walked out of the dining room toward the back of the building. He dialed Bailey's number. There was no answer. Then he texted Patrick. "Good luck tonight. I'm going after Bailey. I'll send a cab for you later."

Once he got in his car, he called out to Bailey. *"Where are you love?"* But he never got a response. He drove to Father Ambrose's church. Maybe Bailey was there with the priest. But the church was locked up and the lights were off. That was unusual unless Father Ambrose was out of town. He tried to call him on his cell, but the priest didn't answer either. He headed to his home. Maybe Bailey was there.

She deserved to be angry. If she had seen the rock Fionnuala was wearing, she would be concerned. But if Fionnuala told her the story she told him, Bailey would be hurt. The truth was, he didn't remember anything that night. And no money was missing from his accounts, so she could have bought the rock herself.

Bailey caught the last plane to the States. She did well to fight back the tears. She had been a fool to think she could have a second chance at love. But the time she spent in Ireland and the love she and Michael made was priceless. She would savor those memories. She could honestly tell her friends at work that she had indeed been kissed by an Irishman. Her two week vacation had turned into at least six weeks and she still didn't see the east coast of Ireland. While she was in flight, she heard Michael call out to her. She tried to ignore his words, but eventually caved in. *"Congratulations on your engagement to Fionnuala. I hope you two will be happy together."*

Michael pulled up to the garage at his home. He found Father Ambrose in his office, waiting for him.

"Father Ambrose! What are you doing here? Where's Bailey?"

"Hello Michael. I came to the banquet hall to speak to you tonight. I had a donation for the clinic, but was told I wasn't invited. I was ordered out of the building with the threat of calling the Garda."

"What? Who did that?"

Father Ambrose handed him a check for Patrick. "Fionnuala. I was escorted out with Bailey."

"No!"

"Fionnuala told us that you and she chose the large ring she flashed at us several times."

"Oh, Lord. I should have stopped it when it started. I just couldn't deal with that woman."

"Well, it's too late, I'm afraid."

"Is Bailey here?"

"No. She's on her way to the States."

Michael rubbed his face. "Father, I want her in my life, permanently."

"Did you tell her as much?"

"I told her she was the only woman I wanted in my life."

"I think she's waiting for a proposal, Michael, and the three words every woman needs to hear on a regular basis."

"What three words?"

"I'll let you figure that out for yourself, Michael."

14

THE PROPOSAL

Michael paced back and forth in his office. He wanted to leave and head for America and bring Bailey back where she belonged but he had too many obligations here. He had depended on her so much that he forgot what it was like to do everything himself. Had he taken advantage of her? Did he get so comfortable with her that she felt...used? Didn't she know he loved her? Then it dawned on him. He called her 'love' but he never told her he loved her. Is that what Father meant? Was he supposed to say, 'I love you?'

In that moment, he knew what he had to do. He called Larry to see if there was anything else he needed to do about the hotel.

"I'll take it from here," Larry said. "I'll send you weekly reports on what the hotel does financially, and monthly, I'll send you a check on your share of the business. You need to get the pictures for the rooms. Bailey said you had some prints that needed to be framed."

"Oh, yes. I'll take care of that tomorrow," Michael said.

He started a list of things to do.

He took Daisy for a walk and mentally planned out the rest of his day. Once Daisy was settled in the house, he drove back to Limerick to pick up Patrick.

Now that he was finished with the hotel, he would concentrate on Patrick's clinic. He had already told Findley he would retire after the clinic was finished. He didn't want to see anyone from the fundraiser. The more he thought of what Fionnuala did, the madder he got. Once he arrived at the location, he drove around the back and texted Patrick to meet him there.

Patrick saw him and walked toward the car.

"Where's Bailey?" Patrick asked. He opened the door and climbed into the car.

"I've lost her son. She's gone back to the States."

"When? What happened?"

He explained what Father Ambrose had told him.

"Damn that woman!" Patrick said.

"Patrick! I'll not hear you talk like that. I'm going to get Bailey back. I need to find her. She means everything to me."

"You never told her you loved her, did you?"

"I thought my actions spoke loud and clear, but Father Ambrose pointed out that she needed to hear me say it. I failed her in that regard."

"Did she say as much to you?" Patrick asked.

"Yes. She told me she loved me when you brought me home from Tullamore. I should have said it to her then."

The ride home from Limerick gave him time to think.

"They collected over $50,000 for the clinic, dad. I have you to thank and then I'll be sending out thank you letters to many people after this."

"How much longer will you be at O'Donnel's?"

"I've given my notice. I'll work another week and then I'll be able to help you with the construction."

"That's grand. I may have you do just that while I fetch the woman I plan to marry."

Once Michael and Patrick returned home, everywhere Michael looked, reminded him of Bailey. The living room, the kitchen, the tub, the empty bed. He went back into the kitchen and found a bottle of scotch. He poured a shot and drank it straight away. This was going to be a hard week for him without Bailey.

Bailey arrived home exhausted. The eight-hour flight from Ireland to New York and then Washington to Knoxville, left her drained. She unpacked then took a long, soaking bath. All her unshed tears came flowing down. She missed Michael. Taking a bubble bath wasn't the same without him. She tried to sleep but tossed and turned, thinking of Michael and Patrick. She left them in a hurry and without a goodbye.

The next day, she called the Hudson Inn for her schedule. Since they weren't expecting her just yet, she wasn't on it. The GM said she would call her back if anyone wanted to switch for this week. In the meantime, she would be added next week to the schedule.

Then, she headed to the Smoky Brewery to pick up her schedule from them. When she returned home, she sent off her manuscript to her editor and contacted her cover artist to have a cover made. She caught up on emails and then called her daughter and sons to let them know she was safely home. The three of them planned a dinner for later in the week.

On her first day back at the Brewery, she looked over a menu when Dee approached her. "It's about time you showed up," Dee said.

"Well, setting up a new hotel in Ireland took longer than I thought. The hotel wasn't finished until recently."

"Really? So let's hear about your travels."

Bailey talked about her brief tour of the west coast of Ireland, leaving out the part about Michael.

"Lord. Well, I'm glad you're back."

"Me, too."

Crystal walked up to the hostess stand. "Hey, did you get kissed by an Irishman?"

"I sure did," she said. She tried to hold back a smile, but it was useless.

"Let's hear it. What happened?" Dee said.

"You can read about it in my latest book."

"What? You're going to make us read about it?" Dee asked.

"Yes, I am."

"I don't read," Crystal said.

The manager walked up to the stand. "Okay girls, look like you're busy or I'm cutting one of you."

Dee headed for her table and Crystal went to the bathroom, while Bailey wiped down some tables.

That was close. She didn't think she could tell anyone the truth without crying. It was all she could do to keep from crying now. She was a big girl and had a big girl fling. She'll laugh about it years from now. She just had to get through 'now'.

Later that night, she finally told Dee what really happened while the servers were counting out their tips and Bailey was waiting for the manager to count her drawer.

"I'm sorry honey. I wish it turned out better for you." Dee gave her a hug.

"Yeah, me too."

The rest of the week, Bailey continued her schedule at the Brewery and then went home to work on another novel. She stopped by the grocery store to pick up some things for her dinner with the kids. She realized, she hadn't cooked since she had been home, unless you count frozen vegetables. Had she eaten this week? She couldn't remember. She had lost her appetite and Michael was constantly on her mind.

He called to her each night, '*Hello, love. Where are you? I miss hearing your voice.*' And each night, she cried herself to sleep.

Dinner with the kids was hard. She tried to tell them about the hotel and all the work that she had seen them do while she trained the new hires. She talked about her short trips with Michael where she got lots of pictures, but she skimmed over some of the parts that related to him. She referred to him as Mr. Shaunnessy and how she helped his son with his new clinic by taking photos of the local people's pets.

The next day, she printed out some of the pictures she had taken and ran across the one of her and Michael. She printed two of those. She put one in a frame and kept it in her bedroom. The other, she put in her purse. She would show that to Dee. All the others, she showed to her kids.

Before heading to work at the Brewery, she found a letter in her mail box from Ireland. Her hand shook when she saw the postmark. Then she read the name, P. Shaunnessy. She quickly opened the letter. It was a thank you card from Patrick.

'*Thank you for all the hard work you did for me, Bailey. I will never forget you.*'

Patrick,

All God's Creatures, Great and Small

She wiped a tear from her eye and set the card on her kitchen table. She headed out to work.

When things slowed down at the Brewery, she pulled out the picture of her and Michael and showed it to Dee.

"Whoa. He's the Irishman who kissed you?" Dee asked.

"Well, yes." She didn't want to admit that they had shared more than a kiss, but when she'd talked to Dee the week before, she alluded to it.

"What?" Tammy overheard what Dee said. "Let me see."

Before she realized it, the girls passed the picture around.

"Hey, I want that picture back," she said.

"It looks like you two did more than kissing," Crystal said.

Bailey felt her face grow hot. "Give me the picture, please."

Crystal handed it back and she put it away.

Since it was slow, Bailey took her sanitizer and went into the bathroom to wipe down the counters. Before she finished, Crystal came into the bathroom.

"There's someone here to see you," Crystal said.

"One of my kids?"

"No." She turned and left.

Bailey washed her hands and brought the sanitizer out with her.

When she stepped up to the hostess stand, there stood Michael. Her heart pounded.

"What are you doing here?" she asked.

"You're a hard woman to find, Bailey Jackson."

"What?" Bailey set the sanitizer on the hostess stand. She realized all her coworkers were standing around, listening.

"I'm taking a break," she announced. Then she grabbed her things in one hand and pulled Michael with her other hand. She led him outside.

"You could have sent me a letter or called me," she said.

"I had to see you, Bailey. I had to tell you I love you."

She covered her mouth with her hand and the tears flowed down her cheeks. "You don't know how long I've wanted to hear that. But what about your fiancé?"

"Fionnuala?"

"Yeah, that's the one." She wiped her eyes with the back of her hand. Michael handed her a handkerchief. She patted her eyes dry.

"I gave her an ultimatum. I told her to call the newspapers and tell them the engagement is broken off, or I would phone the Garda and tell them she drugged me and kidnapped me."

"So she gave in?"

"No. She laughed at me. Then I called the Garda. She's sitting in prison at the moment. Patrick put the notice in the newspapers."

"She didn't believe you?"

"Apparently not."

Bailey laughed. "When you set your mind to do something, you can accomplish a lot."

Michael knelt down on the concrete sidewalk outside the Brewery and took her hand in his. "Bailey Jackson, I love you. I can't live without you. Marry me and make me the happiest man in the world."

"Yes! Michael Patrick Shaunnessy, I'd love to marry you so you can make me the happiest woman in the world."

She pulled him to his feet and embraced him. His hug was warm and comforting. She didn't want to let go.

"Let's get married here, Michael."

"Here on the sidewalk?"

"No, here in Tennessee. We'll be living in Ireland, right?"

"Yes."

"I want you to meet my kids. How much time have you got?"

"This week."

"I guess we have a lot to do in one week."

15

THE WEDDING

Bailey spent the next two days planning her wedding at one of the chapels in Gatlinburg. She invited her coworkers at the Brewery and the Hudson Inn, along with her kids and a few close friends. She also turned in her notice to both places.

Michael stayed with her at her house.

"You'll be keeping this place, won't you, Bailey?" Michael asked.

"Of course. I thought of letting one of my kids live in it to keep it up so we can have a place to visit."

"Brilliant. The only thing this place needs is a bigger tub."

"Or we can just shower together while we are here."

Michael pulled her into a passionate kiss that grew into a trail of kisses down her neck.

"If we keep this up, Michael, I'll be late for work."

"Hmm. We'll have to pick up where we leave off when you get home, then." Michael unbuttoned her blouse.

"Brilliant," Bailey said. She buttoned her blouse back.

"I'll have dinner ready when you get home," Michael said.

"That will be a first for me," she said.

"It won't be the last time, either. I intend to spoil you when I get you home to Ireland."

"It sounds good to me," she said. She gave him a quick kiss and headed off to work.

"I can't believe you found a gorgeous man in Ireland," Tammy said.

Bailey wiped down the hostess stand with the sanitizer. "He was my dream lover."

"Dream lover?"

"Yes. I dreamt about meeting him every night. We kissed, made love, and then it was over."

"You didn't dream anything after that?"

"No, but I got to live my dream while I was in Ireland."

"Live what?" Dee asked. She handed Bailey a stack of menus.

"Technically, I worked for Larry, who owns our Hudson Inn here. He and Michael bought the hotel in Ireland and turned it into another Hudson Inn. That's how I met Michael who turned out to be my dream lover. We both had the same dreams."

"That's hard to believe," Tammy said.

"Well, then, you'll find it even harder to believe he was an angel who decided to become human."

"You're right. I don't believe that either," Tammy said.

"Well, it's true. We've had a spiritual connection through

our dreams, so I can talk to him telepathically and he can talk to me that way."

"Angel or not, that guy is gorgeous," Dee said.

"Thank you," Bailey said. "He is a wonderful man, an architect who loves his son, loves to paint, and buys my books."

"Books? What books?" Tammy asked.

"Didn't you know? Bailey is an author," Dee said.

"No, I didn't."

"Yes, and she wrote a story about all this," Dee said. She made a circular motion to include the Brewery and it's hostesses.

"You'll have to buy my latest book to get the details," Bailey said.

"I want to know why you came back without him. Why was he looking for you?" Crystal asked. She stacked several menus on the hostess stand.

"Unfortunately, a gorgeous redhead came between us. Turns out, she was the one who drugged him and kidnapped him."

"What's this?" Tammy asked.

"I think she was trying to make things hard for me but instead, she brought me and Michael closer together. Quite ironic. I should thank her for that."

"And we have to buy your book to get the details?" Tammy asked.

"Yep."

"So now that you've turned in your notice, when will you be leaving?" Dee asked.

"The day after the wedding. My kids will be coming to Ireland to meet Patrick and visit the place next month."

"Who's Patrick?" Tammy asked.

"That's Michael's son. He's a veterinarian and is opening

a clinic in Roundstone. You're all invited to the wedding, by the way."

Her kids had come over for dinner the night before the wedding, asking Michael all kinds of questions. Michael had an answer for every question they asked. When they felt satisfied with his answers, they gave their approval of him and willingly volunteered to participate in the ceremonies.

The next day, Bailey's daughter, Bridget was her maid of honor, while her eldest son gave her away and her youngest son stood as best man for Michael.

Michael and Bailey stood before the minister and the two of them exchanged the vows they wrote together for the occasion.

When the minister pronounced them husband and wife, all her coworkers cheered.

Afterward, in a nearby restaurant in Gatlinburg, the party commenced. There was music, dancing, and a few people sang, along with cake and liquid refreshments.

"Your coworkers know how to have good craic," Michael said.

"Yes, they do." She realized that was one of the reasons she enjoyed working at the Brewery.

"Bailey, I think this is the happiest day of my life," Michael said. He wrapped his arm around her waist.

"The happiest day of my life was when I discovered you were real, Michael." She touched his cheek with her hand.

"I love you, Bailey Shaunnessy."

"And I love you, Michael Shaunnessy. Forever and ever."

DARK DEMON

CHAPTER ONE

Elena Romero Cummings, Miami-Dade Police Department Detective, glanced at her notes, then spoke to Keith from the tech team. "Got anything, Keith?"

She stood in the middle of a small repair shop in downtown Miami. The shop owner called when he came to open up for business and discovered he had been robbed. Keith worked on the register, while Danny worked on the door facing, trying to get fingerprints. Amanda photographed footprints.

"I might have a print we can work with. Whoever did this was good," Keith said.

There hadn't been much damage except at the doorway. It appeared to be ripped open with a crowbar. And the register was not damaged. They either worked here or knew something about registers.

Pete Cummings, her husband and partner, walked up to her.

"They didn't have an alarm system and only took money from the register," he said.

"This one is a little tougher, Pete. Keith may have a print, but I'm not getting my hopes up."

"There's something else." He leaned in to whisper.

She glanced up at his tall frame. Pete glanced around the small shop, a scowl on his face. "I smell a demon."

"A demon? Like in Satan?"

"Yes. This may have been done by a human, but there was a demon in this store."

"Well, that's a first. I've never hunted a demon before."

"I pray we never have to, Elena."

She got the owner's phone number and left him her card. She realized she would have to change the card and add her new married name. She smiled at the thought.

"Did you get a look outside, Pete?" she asked.

"Yes, but it looks like they left through the front door. I mentioned it to Keith. He said he'd check everything before he left."

The two left the shop and headed for Pete's truck. He opened the door for her and she climbed up inside. He headed back to the station when they got another call on the radio.

"Unit 19, come in," the dispatcher said.

She grabbed the radio and keyed the mike. "This is Unit 19, go ahead," she said.

"We've got another robbery near your location. Can you copy?"

She flipped open her notebook and grabbed a pen. "Go ahead."

The dispatcher gave her the address and she wrote it down.

"We're enroute, Unit 19, out," she said. Elena put the radio back in it's holder, and gave Pete the address.

He turned the truck around and then headed to the new address. "It's only a block away from the first break-in."

"Two break-ins on the same day," she said.

"I wonder if we're dealing with the same people since it's so close to the other one," Pete said.

"That's what I'm thinking, too, Pete."

"That's what I like about working with you, Elena. We think a lot alike."

"I know. That's why I've been putting off telling the Captain we're married."

He glanced her way. "You're thinking he'll separate us, aren't you?"

"I know he will. I just hope we're on the same schedule."

"I hope he doesn't leave you without a partner," Pete said.

"Yeah, me, too." She reached out and touched his arm. She liked touching him. It gave her strength.

Pete pulled up to the second store and managed to open Elena's door before she did it herself. She loved that about him and the fact he once was an angel.

Elena grabbed the portable radio and clipped it to her belt. Then she touched Pete's cheek. "Thank you, Pete."

He helped her down and locked up. The two of them headed to the shop where the owner greeted them at the door.

Elena flashed her badge. Pete wore his on his belt.

"Are you the owner?" she asked.

"Yes. I went to open my store and realized it was already opened.

"What can you tell us about what's happened?" she asked.

"The door was pried open. The facing was damaged," he said.

Pete looked over her shoulder at the gouged out wood.

The owner used some napkins to open the door for them. He lead them to the register.

"Do you always leave the drawer open?" she asked.

"Yes, but the money is in the safe." The owner showed them to the office. "I usually leave the money locked in the safe over there," he pointed to a wall. A wall with a big hole in it.

"Oh, my. I take it that hole wasn't here when you left, was it?"

"No. There was no hole yesterday."

"Was anything else taken?" Pete asked.

"I don't think so. I haven't done an inventory yet, just glanced around.

Elena wrote down what the owner said, along with notes about the entrance.

"Did you see anything yourself?" Pete asked.

"No. I wish I had."

Pete called the tech team on the radio and let them know about this store as well.

"They'll be here shortly," Pete said.

"I guess we can wait until they get here," Elena said.

Pete shook his head."

"What is it?"

"I smell the same demon in this place," Pete said. He walked around the store, looking things over. "Can I see the office again."

"Help yourself," the owner said.

Pete remained in the office a few minutes, while she asked the owner more questions. "Did you recently hire anyone new?"

"No. I've had the same crew here for years. I pay them well so they will stay."

"Anyone acting different lately?"

He thought for a moment. "I don't think so."

"Anything unusual happen here, lately?"

He thought again. "I do remember a gentleman trying to sell me a security system. I have never had any problems before so I refused. He was very pushy."

"Do you remember who he was?"

"He left a card. It's in my office." The owner headed to the office to retrieve it and passed Pete.

Pete whispered to her. "The smell is the strongest in his office."

The owner returned with the card. About the same time, some of the tech team and a police unit showed up.

Pete let them inside and they began working on the entrance.

"Do you have another entrance?" she asked.

"Yes." The owner led them to the back door. It was unlocked and ajar.

"Did you come in this way?"

"I did not."

Pete headed to the front of the store, while she looked around outside. The gravel in the back looked disturbed. She would have to alert the tech team to that fact. Before she could head back inside, Juan, one of the team members, joined her.

"We found some tire prints at the first shop. Since this is gravel, I'm not sure what we can find, but we'll get on it."

"Thanks."

The dispatcher called on the radio. Another robbery was reported. Before she could answer, she heard Pete's voice come across the radio.

Pete popped his head out the door. "We got another call."

She joined him and they both headed out the front door. It was down the street.

"I'll walk," she said. Pete moved his truck to the end of the block.

He waited for her and the two met the owner outside his door.

"That was fast," the owner said.

"Your neighbor down the street had a visitor as well," she said.

"Excuse us, just a minute," Pete said. He turned toward her, moving her away from the shop owner.

"Elena, that demon smell is on you," he said. He sniffed her hair.

"On me? How did that happen?"

"Did you touch something in that last shop?"

She thought about what had transpired. "The owner gave me a card." She pulled it out of her back pocket of her jeans and showed it to him.

"Drop it."

"What? I need the information."

"Write it down and throw that card away. Do it now."

She pulled out her notebook and copied the name and phone number. Then tossed the card into a trash receptacle on the sidewalk.

Pete handed her some sanitizer and she rubbed it on her hands, the pen, and the front of the notebook. "Do you still smell it?"

He sniffed her hands. "I think you got it."

"What was that all about?" she asked.

"I wouldn't want him to track you. Plus it's an overwhelming scent."

"Hmm." She followed Pete inside, where the owner had been waiting. Maybe it would distract him from any new demon scent, she thought.

"Sorry about that," she apologized. She glanced around the shop. "What kind of store is this?"

"We sell parts for electronics, small appliances or small engines."

"Anything missing?" Pete asked.

"So far, just money from the register. If anything else turns up, I'll contact you," the owner said.

Elena pulled out her card and handed it to him. "You can reach us at this number," she said.

"We have a tech team down the street. They'll be here shortly," Pete said.

"Have you experienced anything unusual lately, besides this break-in?" she asked.

"Yes. I had a customer come in and suggest I get a security system. He was quite pushy about it and made me feel uncomfortable."

"Did he leave his card?" she asked.

"He wanted to, but I refused it. I didn't like the way he talked to me."

"What way was that?" Pete asked.

"Kind of threatening, like something could happen if I didn't get a security system in place."

"Do you think you would recognize him if you saw him again?" she asked.

"I think so."

"Our tech team has an artist that could draw him from your description," she said.

"Really? I would like to see if they can do that."

"Can you show me where this person was when you talked to him?" Pete asked.

"Right here," he pointed to the register.

"And where were you?" Elena asked.

The owner walked around to the register on the counter. "I stood here, facing him. He stood where you are," he said.

Pete reached out and touched the man's shoulder. "I want

you to think about what he looked like when you talked to him."

"Sure. He said 'it looks like you don't have a security system in here.'"

"And what did you say?" Elena asked.

"I really don't need one. Then he smirked and said, 'yes, you do.'"

"Thank you," Pete said, removing his hand from the owner's shoulder.

"Do you have a back door?" Elena asked.

"Yes." He pointed in the direction.

"We'll take a look while we wait for the tech team," she said.

She followed Pete out the door.

"I saw him, Elena. I saw the demon."

"Did you smell him as well?"

"Yes. The scent was strong in that spot."

"What kind of demon are we looking for?"

"He's passing himself off as human. He's good looking, sharply dressed. I'll have to reach out to other spirit beings to see who he is. I'm not familiar with him."

"How do we fight a demon?"

"This calls for a spiritual battle, Elena. I just don't know if I can protect you from him."

"There must be some way. Wouldn't prayers help?"

"Yes. You know how to put on the armor of God, right?"

"Yes."

"Do it now. We'll both do it." Pete closed his eyes in prayer, and she did the same thing, reciting Ephesians 6:10-17.

She made the motions, putting on the belt of truth around her waist. Then she made the motion of putting on her breast-plate of righteousness. She clicked her heels together to be ready to spread the gospel of truth. Then she made the motion of a large shield of faith that was as tall as she was to put out the burning arrows of the evil one. Finally, she donned the helmet of salvation and raised her hand as if she held a sword of the Spirit.

"I'm ready," she said.

"We've got to do this every day," he said. He blinked and they were both physically wearing the armor of God.

"Wow! This shield of faith is really heavy," she said. "And can you teach me how to wield this sword?"

"It takes a lot of practice, but yes, I will teach you," Pete said.

Just then, Amanda from the tech team came out the door.

"What in the world are you two wearing?" she asked.

"We're wearing the armor of God," Elena said.

"Ok? I need to photograph this area for Keith," Amanda said.

"Sure. It's all clear," Elena said. She headed toward the door and Pete followed her. As they stepped through the doorway, he blinked and the armor disappeared.

"Are we still wearing our armor, spiritually?" she whispered.

"Yes. I wanted you to see what the evil spirits see when we wear it," he whispered back.

"Oh. Well, that is cool."

She spent a few minutes updating Keith when her stomach growled. She glanced at her watch and realized it was after twelve. If she was hungry, she knew Pete was starving. She wrapped up with Keith and found Pete talking to the owner once more. Pete handed the owner her card. Since Pete was still new to the detective division, he didn't have any business cards, so he carried hers. That's another thing she would have to do once she spoke to the Captain. She waited beside Pete and when he finished, they walked out to his truck.

"Where are we having lunch?" she asked.

"Somewhere close. I'm starving," he said.

"There's a sandwich shop over there. Let's try that one," she said.

They walked together across the street and went inside the 'Little Sandwich Shop.'

There was a line at the counter. She glanced around the small shop. There were a few small tables with two seats at each one. Since there were many offices downtown, people must buy the sandwiches and take them back to work, she thought.

She noticed the menu was on a large chalkboard on the wall behind the counter. There were two women working. One was taking orders and ringing up the sales, while the other made the sandwiches.

"I'll take the ham and Swiss wrap with a bottle of water," Pete said. "How about you, Elena? What'll you have?"

"That sounds good. I'll have the same, please," she said.

Pete paid for their sandwiches while she watched the two women. The blonde woman ringing up their purchases had gorgeous skin coloring with a Mediterranean look about her. Her green eyes sparkled when she smiled. The Hispanic woman preparing the food was young and pretty as well, but her eyes were dark brown with a beautiful caramel coloring. The two women joked as they worked, making it fun to listen to them.

"How long has your shop been open?" she asked.

"Oh, we've been here about four years now," the blonde said. "I'm Alona Gabriel, the owner," she said. "And this is my loyal employee, Teresa."

"Nice to meet you," Elena said.

"You haven't had any trouble here lately, have you?" Pete asked.

"No. Why do you ask?"

"We just worked three robberies in this neighborhood," Elena said.

"Worked?" Alona asked.

"We're detectives for the Miami-Dade Police Department," Elena said, showing her badge.

"Oh? No. We haven't had any problems." Alona handed her the two bottles of water.

"Thank you," Elena said. "If you have anyone asking you about security, would you call us?" she asked.

Teresa brought their wraps to them, and Elena handed Alona her card.

"Do you want to eat here?" Pete asked her.

"Sure, why not?" They sat at a table with a view of the street. Another couple sat a table away.

Pete bit into his wrap before she could remove the paper from hers. "You really were hungry, weren't you?"

He nodded.

"This is really good. I was hungrier than I thought," she said. By the time they finished, it was a little after one.

"We need to head back to the office and type up our reports," she said.

"Maybe Keith will have something by then," Pete said.

"I hope so. If we're dealing with professionals, it may be hard to figure this one out."

"Especially if a demon is involved," he whispered.

They walked outside into the Florida sunshine and crossed the street to get to Pete's truck.

"I didn't want to say anything inside the sandwich shop, but I felt the presence of a spiritual being of some sort," Pete said. He opened Elena's door.

"A spiritual being? Like an angel?" She stopped half way inside the truck.

"I'm not sure. I've never felt that presence before."

She sat on the seat and put her hand on Pete's shoulder.

"But not a demon?"

"No. Definitely not a demon."

He closed the door and walked around to his side of the truck.

"What have we gotten ourselves into, Pete?"

"I hope it's just a robbery, but I have a feeling it's more than that from what we've found out so far."

"You know, we may need to go back to the second shop and have you touch the owner to see if he can remember the security hustler," she said.

"You're probably right. After we get these reports done, we can check back if we have time."

They each took a report and worked on it to finish faster. Then they exchanged the reports and added their own notes to complete them. The third one, they worked on together. Before they could finish the last report, they had another call. This one was a little different.

"This is a neighborhood not too far from downtown," she said. She glanced at the address, then handed it to Pete.

It was almost four when they arrived. A police unit was already there. One officer stood outside a townhouse on the sidewalk. He kept the crowd of people away from the unit.

She showed him her badge. "Miami-Dade, robbery division," she said.

"What can you tell us, officer?" Pete asked.

"The couple inside were watching t.v. when two men barged through the door and accosted them. Officer Sanchez is inside, interviewing the wife."

"Did you speak to either of them?" she asked.

"I interviewed the husband," he said. He glanced at his notes and repeated what he had written down. She took her own notes from what he had gotten, and wrote down his name, Officer Wentworth. "Thank you." She turned to Pete and realized he wasn't beside her.

When she glanced around, she saw Pete petting a brown dog beside Alona Gabriel.